# SEAL STORY

Other Kelpies by the same author

THE DESPERATE JOURNEY
ESCAPE IN DARKNESS
FLASH THE SHEEPDOG
TURK THE BORDER COLLIE
HAKI THE SHETLAND PONY

If you liked this story then why not look out for other Kelpies. There are dozens of stories to choose from : ghosts, spy stories, animals and the countryside, witches, mysteries and secrets, adventures and many more. Kelpie paperbacks are available from all good bookshops.

For your free Kelpie badge and complete catalogue please send a stamped addressed envelope to:
Margaret Ritchie (K.C.B.),
Canongate Publishing Ltd.,
17 Jeffrey Street, Edinburgh
EH1 1DR.

# SEAL STORY

## Kathleen Fidler

*Illustrated by Douglas Phillips*

**CANONGATE • KELPIES**

First published 1979 by Lutterworth Press
First published in Kelpies 1988


© 1979 Kathleen Fidler


Cover illustration by Alexa Rutherford


Printed in Great Britain
by Cox & Wyman Ltd, Reading


ISBN 0 86241 195 5

CANONGATE PUBLISHING LTD
17 JEFFREY STREET, EDINBURGH EH1 1DR

*For my dear friend*
*Barbara F. McKenzie*

With my thanks to Miss M. A. M. Gordon
who went with me to Lindisfarne

# Contents

It was Friday afternoon and out of the little island school of Lindisfarne came tumbling the twenty pupils, their lessons over for the week after their final singing period. They were eager to get home to tea for it was a chill November day and already the mists were beginning to form over the sand flats as the tide swept up towards the island.

"Hi there, young Reid!" a big, red-headed boy called, barring the way of a smaller, stockily-built lad. "What's your hurry? What about a game of football?"

"Who with?" Aidan Reid asked.

"Me, of course, and Bill Cromarty and Joe Bell. We need another lad."

"If you mean to kick a football round the streets of the town, no, I'm not coming. That's not football, Tom Watson. Football needs a team."

"You know we haven't boys enough in the school to make a team. There won't be a proper football team till we go to the mainland school."

"I'll wait till then." Aidan Reid tried to edge his way round the group of three boys, but Tom Watson put out an arm to stop him.

"A right ninny you'll look when you get to the other school and you can't even kick a ball straight!" Tom Watson jeered. "But you *are* a soppy kid, Aidan Reid! You've got a right soppy name, too, *Aidan*! Oh, I know you try to hide it by calling yourself Dan for short. But when we get to the school at Tweedmouth, I'll tell everyone what a daft name you've got!"

Aidan Reid went red with anger.

"Look at the silly kid's red face!" Tom Watson tormented him. "He'll be scared stiff when he gets to the mainland school. The only things he knows anything about are birds and fish." Tom Watson pretended to sniff the air. "Fish! Can't you smell rotten stinking fish, lads?" The other boys laughed a little uneasily. "Oh! The smell comes off *you*, Aidan Reid!" Tom Watson sneered. "You'd think he lived in a lobster pot down by the harbour there!"

'I don't stink of fish. I'm cleaner than you, Tom Watson!" Aidan Reid was goaded into replying. "And fishing's a good trade anyway, better than what *your* father does, keeping an ice-cream shop!"

Tom Watson's father had a chain of ice-cream vans, operating on the mainland as well as on the island.

"Don't you cheek me!" Tom Watson advanced with uplifted fist, but he stopped short when he saw Aidan had squared up his fists too. Tom took a step backwards.

"Come on, lads! He's not worth bothering about."

Tom Watson took a small transistor radio from his pocket and switched it on, to a high-pitched "pop" tune. "I'll bet *your* father can't afford to give you one of these! I could hold it in one hand and fight you with the other."

Tom Watson might have been called upon to make good his boast, but Bill Cromarty, who had been keeping a wary eye on the school gate, called, "Watch out! Teacher's coming!"

"I'll get you one of these days, all the same, young Reid!" Tom Watson called after Dan.

The little group scattered. Tom Watson and his friends

went down Marygate, the radio blaring loudly and bringing folk to their windows, while Aidan Reid ran down Prior Lane towards the Market Place.

Aidan swallowed down the lump in his throat. He hated Tom Watson for a bully—and for jeering at his name. Come to that, Aidan didn't like his name either! Why couldn't his parents have christened him just Dan, seeing that was the name most people gave him? Only his grandmother always called him Aidan. As for Tom Watson's sneer about fishing, Aidan cared nothing for that. He was proud of his father and their fishing-coble, the "Jenny", but he wished he could have a transistor radio too and be "upsides" with Tom Watson. Perhaps, some day, if the fishing was good...

Aidan Reid was nine years old. He was blue-eyed and fairhaired, sturdily built in his navy fisherman's jersey. His grandmother had knitted it in one of the intricate Shetland patterns, for she had been a Shetlander until she came to Lindisfarne off the coast of Northumberland. Lindisfarne is

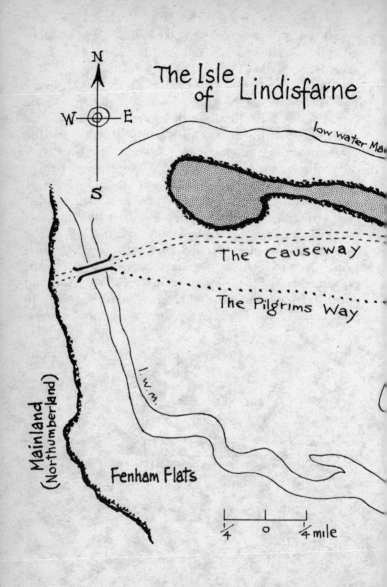

The Isle
of Lindisfarne

low water Ma

The Causeway

The Pilgrims Way

l.w.m.

Mainland (Northumberland)

Fenham Flats

¼   0   ¼ mile

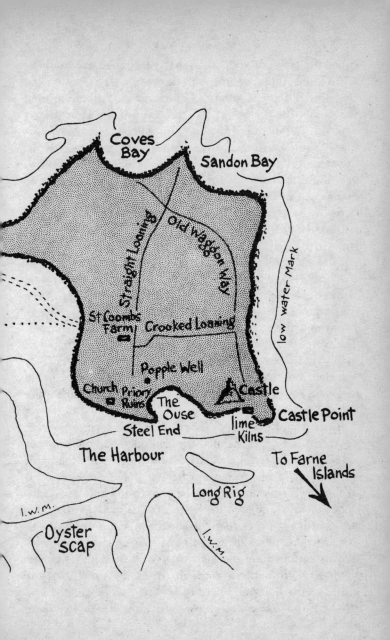

called the "Holy Island", though it is only an island for about seven hours a day when the tides sweep over the causeway that joins it to the mainland. Centuries ago, pilgrims crossed the sandy flats on foot at low tide to visit the Holy Island where St Aidan and St Cuthbert once lived; nowadays, during the summer, tourists drive in a constant procession across the causeway to the island. Folk come from far and near to visit Lindisfarne: to see the Priory built by the Benedictine monks nearly a thousand years ago, on the site of St Cuthbert's monastery which was burned by Danish raiders; to admire the reproductions of the Lindisfarne Gospels which were written by the monks soon after St Cuthbert's death, and which are now treasured in the British Museum; and to climb the cobbled way that winds upwards to fairytale Beblowe Castle, perched on a rocky hill at the end of the island and looking as if it grew there.

But now it was November and the tourists had departed. The car park was closed, and there was no tinkle of tea-cups in the cottage tea-rooms, no crowds in the inn-parlours. This was the time that Aidan liked best, when the island home he loved, sometimes shrouded in mist, belonged once more only to its people.

Aidan's family had been fisherfolk of Lindisfarne for many generations. In earlier times, the fishermen had gone far out to sea after the herring shoals, but now the fishing was almost all "inshore", and Aidan's father set pots for lobsters and drift nets for salmon. The big herring cobles had lain abandoned on the shore until the fishermen stripped them of their inside fittings, turned them upside down, cut doors in them, and used them for storing their gear. There they stood now like mysterious giant black relics of the past. Aidan's father, Peter Reid, owned one of them. In earlier times, too, the old "herring houses" where the herring were smoked and turned into kippers stood close to the foreshore. Now these houses, and many of the fishermen's cottages, too, had been altered to make holiday homes; the Reids, though, still lived in one of the old red-tiled cottages on the road round Ouse Bay which led to Steel End and the Harbour.

There were several narrow lanes by which Aidan Reid could go home, but on this particular afternoon he had to call at the shop in the Market Place to get a newspaper for

his grandfather. The newspaper delivery was late today because the tide had been up during the morning, cutting off Lindisfarne from the mainland.

"Tell your Grandma that the new knitting-wool came in today, Dan. She was asking me about it last week," Mrs Kerr, the shopkeeper, told him. Her shop sold everything from shell souvenirs to soap, from basins to biscuits.

"I'll remember," Dan promised.

Already the November mist was gathering round him as he ran along Fenkle Street and by St Cuthbert's Square to

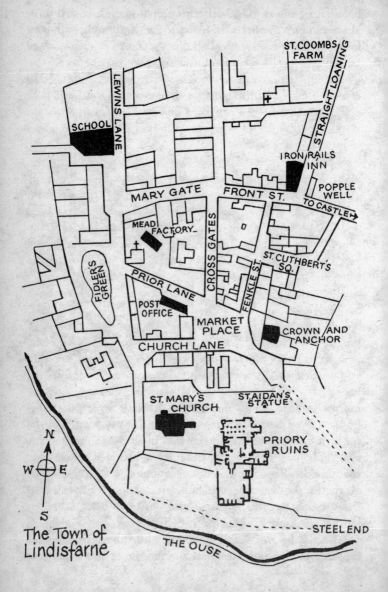

The Town of Lindisfarne

his home. He was glad Mrs Kerr called him Dan. His forehead wrinkled in a puzzled frown as he wondered again why his grandmother always called him Aidan, in full. Of course, Dan was short for Aidan, he knew that; all the same, he wished his grandmother would call him Dan, too. Aidan sounded such a fancy name, the name of the saint whose statue stood by the Priory. Maybe his grandfather could persuade his grandmother to call him Dan, if he asked him.

A good smell of cooking greeted him when he opened the door. On Friday nights Grandma Reid always made fish pie and baked scones and baps for his sister Kate's return from the school on the mainland. The island children only stayed at the Lindisfarne school till they were approaching ten years old. Then they became weekly boarders in a school hostel at Tweedmouth on the mainland. On Mondays a minibus took them over the causeway the twelve miles to Tweedmouth, and on Fridays it brought them back again.

Dan missed Kate very much. He wished she was back with him at the village school, for each time she came home she seemed to have grown a bit away from him, and her talk was all of life on the mainland. Dan did *not* look forward to the time when he too would cross the causeway to the mainland and the Tweedmouth school. He hated the thought of leaving his island with the sound and smell of the sea always at his door, and the wild birds that thronged the sand flats, just as they had done for centuries. People said that thirteen hundred years earlier, when St Cuthbert lived on the island, the eider ducks would come to his call and crowd about his feet. They were still called "St Cuthbert's Ducks" on Lindisfarne. Dan knew them all: the wild geese and the wader birds, the whoopers and the mute swans at the edge of the tide. He knew the haunts of the seals, too, on the sand-banks of the Long Rig and the Oyster Scap facing the harbour.

Sometimes Dan went out with his father in the lobster boat "Jenny" and they passed close by the Farne Islands where the grey seals bred in great numbers. The seals lay close together on the rocks and warily watched the passing boats with their large beautiful eyes. If the boats ventured in too close, some of the younger seals would dive into the water and keep popping up inquisitive heads to look at the humans. The older seals were not so disturbed by visitors; they shifted a little, and one might raise a restless flipper, that was all. Dan wondered a lot about the seals. Grandma Reid would sometimes tell strange mysterious tales about them and how they were really like people in their ways. Perhaps she might be persuaded to tell them a tale about the seals this evening after supper? Friday night was story-telling night when Kate was home.

Dan rushed into the kitchen off the living-room. "There's Grandpa's paper and Mrs Kerr says the new knitting-wool's in and has Kate come?" he cried all in one breath.

"Mercy me, Aidan! You come in like a whirlwind. No, Kate's not here yet."

"But I saw the school bus at Cambridge Corner as I came past."

"Ah, weel, maybe she's called at the mead factory for your mother." Grandma Reid cast a glance at the clock, an old "wag-at-the-wall" with its swinging pendulum. "They'll no' be long. You can be setting the table for supper while you're waiting."

Grandma Reid was active and energetic and she loved cooking and baking, so Dan's mother had declared there was not enough work in the cottage for two women, and she had taken a part-time job at the one small factory on Lindisfarne, which made a drink called mead, and also sold island honey, marmalade and souvenirs to the tourists. Her earnings helped the household, too, if the fishing season was bad.

Dan went about setting the table in the living-room. He glanced through the window at the little bay. The tide had dropped now and his father's coble, the "Jenny", named after Dan's mother, lay moored to the stone jetty at Steel End. Their catch of lobsters had already been boxed and would be taken over to Berwick, to be sent to London by train that night. Most of the catch was sold to the London hotels by the fishing co-operative agency which handled the fishermen's catches. Dan's father and grandfather were walking along the stone pier together. A few minutes more and they would be home, tired and hungry.

"They're coming from the boat," Dan called to his grandmother.

"All's ready for them," she said with satisfaction.

Just then there was the sound of feet along the cobbled road, the door opened, and in came Kate and her mother.

"Hullo, Gran!" Kate said, rushing into the kitchen and giving her grandmother a hug. "I'm back!"

"The racket you make tells me that," her Grandma replied, but there was a warmth in the return hug she gave Kate. "My, though, but it's quiet without you during the week!"

"It'll be quieter still next term when Dan goes to the mainland school too," Jenny Reid reminded her. "Two less to cook for, Grandma!"

"I'm no' exactly looking forward to that," Grandma replied. "I like the bustle o' the bairns about me."

Dan frowned. He was not looking forward to leaving his island either.

"Don't look so bothered, Dan!" his sister told him. "You'll like it at the big school over there. Why! The Hostel's called St Aidan's! It might be named after you."

Dan frowned even more, but Kate went on, "You'll be able to play football there. There were never enough boys at the island school to make up a team."

"I'm not that keen on football," Dan told her. "I'd rather go fishing."

"Stop arguing, you two! Wash your hands and then you can help Grandma to carry the supper in. There's your father and Grandpa at the door now," their mother said.

Obediently they washed their hands at the stone sink in the kitchen. In another moment, their grandfather and their father would be doing the same thing. Grandma insisted on this ritual for old and young alike.

Soon the meal was on the table and the news of the week was cheerfully exchanged.

"What d'you know? I'm to be the chief angel in the Christmas play at school," Kate told them proudly.

"*You* an angel!" Dan mocked her.

"Something you'd never be!" Kate retorted. "Though if you were at the school, they might have you for a shepherd."

"I'd rather be a fisherman," Dan replied stoutly.

Grandpa Reid and Grandma exchanged quiet glances. "Ah, weel, there were fishermen in the Bible too," Grandma said.

"It's fun getting up plays and having a *real* stage at school," Kate said.

"Oh, but we get up plays at our school too," Dan reminded her. "We gave a play at the last Harvest Festival."

"But that wasn't a big play with lots of people in it, like the one we gave when I was a witch, at Hallowe'en."

"Maybe you made a better witch than you will an angel," Dan teased her.

Kate might have retaliated but their father ordered, "Get on with your suppers and stop arguing!" He changed the

said as she knitted away. "Fine it was to see them lying stretched on the rocks in the sunshine. Let a boat go too near, though, and plop! into the water they plunged. But they soon popped their heads out of the waves again and looked around to see the boat, for selkies are right inquisitive creatures."

"I know that." Dan nodded. "I've seen them looking at us when I've been out with Father in the boat to set the lobster pots. Harry Cromarty told me that seals could *sing*. Is it true, Grandma?"

"Weel, I canna' say I've heard them ma'sel'," Grandma replied candidly. "But that's no' to say they don't sing. There's something no' quite canny about them, something almost human. In the islands it was said that after sunset

the selkies cast off their skins and turned into folk. They had
to put their skins on again by sunrise or they could never
go back to live in the sea. But there was one selkie woman
left her sealskin lying on a rock while she sat on the sand
combing her long yellow hair. She didna' notice but when
the great seventh wave came, the wave that is always the
biggest, it swept her sealskin off the rock." Grandma paused
for a moment to adjust her needles and wool.

"Go on, Grandma!" Dan urged her.

"There was a fisher-laddie in his boat round the other
side of the rock and he saw the sealskin and pulled it out
of the water. He said to himself, 'If the skin belongs to a selkie,
that selkie canna' go back to the sea without it. I'll up and
hide the skin in the rafters o' my cottage roof.' And so he
did. Weel, just as he was coming back from his cottage on
the shore he heard a cry. There was a lovely white-skinned
lass calling to him. 'Fisherman, I saw you take my skin.
Please give it back to me, for I cannot live in the sea without
it.'

"She was very beautiful and the fisherman fell in love with
her. He begged her to stay on the land and be his wife. He
would not give back the sealskin to her, nor would he tell
her where he had hidden it, so she had to stay and marry
him."

"Did they live happily ever after?" Kate asked.

"Weel, we might say they did for a time, for the seal-lass
made him a very good wife, and they had seven bonnie children. She seemed happy enough, but she aye cast a longing
glance at the sea and sang a strange sad song that no one
had ever heard before. She never forgot her seal-folk who
lived under the sea and she was homesick for them."

Grandma Reid paused again to fasten on a fresh ball of
wool.

"*Do* go on, Grandma!" Dan begged.

"Wheesht, now! Dinna' be in such a hurry!" she chided him, but with a smile. "Weel, there came a day when the fisherman of Wastness went fishing with his sons while two daughters went gathering limpets for bait for his fish-hooks."

Dan nodded. He knew all about baiting fish-hooks for lobster pots.

"There was one wee lassie left behind," Grandma went on. "She had cut her foot. The mother began looking round the cottage for a piece of rabbit skin to make her a soft slipper.

" 'I know where there's a skin, but it's a seal skin,' the wee girl told her mother.

" 'Where? Where?' the seal wife asked eagerly.

" 'I saw my father lift a skin from the rafters in the roof, look at it, then put it back.'

"The seal wife rushed to get a ladder and climbed up to the roof rafters. There, tucked in under the thatched roof, was the sealskin. It was her own sealskin! She wept for joy and kissed her wee daughter, then cried, 'Goodbye, peerie buddo.' "

"What does that mean?" Kate asked.

" 'Peerie buddo'? Little darling, for sure. I am forgetting that you do not know the old Shetland tongue. And then ...' "

Again Grandma paused.

"And then?" Dan prompted her.

"And then she put on the sealskin and rushed to the shore and plunged into the waves with a wild cry."

"Was she drowned?" Dan asked, his eyes full of concern.

"No, no! She was wearing the sealskin. As the little lass watched, she saw a number o' selkies swimming towards her seal mother, uttering cries o' joy. At least, the wee lassie thought they must be seals, but she was not sure—they were sea *people*, she said, from under the waves. And the seal wife went swimming away with them far to the west."

"And did she ever come back again?" Kate asked.

"No. The call of the sea was too strong for her. That was the last the fisherman ever saw of his lovely seal wife."

Dan stared thoughtfully into the fire. "Are the seals really sea *people*?" he asked.

"Some folk think they are: some folk say they are not," Grandma replied with a mysterious nod.

"But if they're people, then it's wrong to kill them as the slaughter men do at the Farne Islands—as they're going to do right now!" Dan exclaimed indignantly.

"Now, Mother, don't go putting nonsense into the boy's head." Peter Reid, Dan's father, looked up from his newspaper. "We all know the seals are not people."

"That's as may be. That's as a body chooses to think. What is the harm in telling the laddie the old stories?"

"I don't want him to get wrong ideas about the culling, that's all. We're fisherfolk, and we know that the seals eat fish, especially salmon, and that they have to be kept down if we want to earn our living."

Grandpa Reid looked from his son to his wife and shook his head warningly. She rose with dignity and packed her knitting needles into her belt. "I will be making the porridge for breakfast," she said. "I will not be arguing in front of the children."

"Och! There's no argument!" her son said, a little impatiently. "I'm off out to see to the baiting of the lobster pots for the morn's fishing."

The door closed behind him. Grandma Reid was clattering the pans in the back-kitchen. Dan turned to his grandfather. "Is it right or wrong to kill the seals, Grandpa?"

"There are two sides to every question, Dan, as you'll learn when you grow older. We fishermen know the seals eat the salmon, and as you're well aware, Dan, it's by the salmon and lobster fishing that we make our living."

Dan nodded.

"There's not a lot of room on the Farne Islands for the seals that live there, either, nor food enough for them," Grandpa went on, explaining patiently to the boy. "Many of the seals are thin and starved. So it's been decided that it will be for their own good, as well as ours, if the seal herds are cut down in size. That's why the men kill a number of seal calves at the culling."

"But it's cruel!" Dan protested.

"The men who slaughter the seals do it as painlessly as

possible. They use special rifles and they are good marksmen."

"I still wish the seals hadn't to be shot. They're so beautiful when they swim. They look so friendly, too."

"Aye, laddie, that's true enough. They're bonnie creatures."

"Grandma thinks they *might* be people, doesn't she?"

Grandpa Reid laughed. "She brought some fanciful tales with her when she came from the Shetland Isles, Dan. Mind, now, I'm not saying they're wrong, but in the long winter nights in Shetland, the folk there tell each other the old stories over and over again. When a story is repeated often enough, it begins to sound real."

Kate was looking thoughtful too. "How was it Grandma came to Lindisfarne when Shetland is so far away?"

"Why, she came here, of course, when I married her, lassie."

"Yes, but how did you meet her?" Kate persisted.

Her grandfather laughed. "My, my, Kate! What questions you do ask, to be sure! It was when I was a fisherman on a herring-trawler. The Reids were not always in-shore fishermen catching lobster and salmon, you know. In the old days the fishing-boats from Lindisfarne went for the deep-sea fishing too. Well, one day we put into Eyemouth with a catch of herring, and your grandmother was there."

"But what was she doing there?" Kate wanted to know.

"Gutting and packing the herring, of course!" Grandpa Reid seemed surprised Kate did not know. "The herring travelled in shoals down the North Sea and the herring-boats went after them. The Scottish fisher-lassies followed the boats from port to port along the east coast. Then, when we came in with the catches, the women were ready to gut the fish and pack them in salt, ready to be sent, barrel after barrel of them, to Holland and Germany—aye, and to Russia too. There was a great trade in salt herring in those days."

Grandfather Reid puffed at his pipe for a minute, remembering.

"Your Grandma was one of the bonniest o' all the lassies," he said. "When I first saw her, her arms were up to the elbows in brine and right cold it was, but she was singing away like a lintie, leading all the rest of them. I was fair scared to speak to her, though."

"But you did!" Kate laughed.

"Aye, I wished her the time o' day. I feared she might think I was impudent and turn away, but she didna'. She gave me a shy smile and that was the beginning of it. The next herring season we were married and I brought her home to Lindisfarne. Now, any more questions, Kate and Dan?" the old man chuckled.

"Just one, Grandpa. Why does Grandma always call me Aidan, when *you* call me Dan?"

"Surely you'll have learned something of the history of our island? You'll have heard of St Aidan?"

"Well, yes. We learned about him at School. And there's his statue near the Parish Church."

"Don't tell me Dan's called after a *saint*!" Kate pulled a cheeky face at Dan.

"Strange though it may seem to you, Kate, he is! It's the name your grandmother chose for him when he was christened at St Mary's Church. Yes, your mother and father said she should have the naming of him, and right pleased she was." Grandpa smiled at Jenny Reid. "And it's an honour to bear the name for St Aidan was the fine man who brought Christianity to the island—and to all the people of Northumberland. He built the first church here on the island."

"Our school hostel at Tweedmouth is named after him," Kate said thoughtfully. "Where did he come from?"

"From Iona, a little island off the west coast of Scotland. Maybe he settled here because Lindisfarne was a bit like his Scottish home. Maybe because he came from Scotland too, your Grandma wanted you called Aidan."

Dan nodded. He asked an unexpected question. "Did St Aidan love the island and the birds and the seals, then?"

"He must have done, for he spent the rest of his life here. You can think of him climbing the Castle Crag—though it wouldna have had that name then, for there was no castle there in his day. He could gaze over the island and the bay and listen to the tide gurgling over the sand. Maybe he watched the birds just as you do, Dan, the wild geese and the eider ducks, the gulls and the puffins, cormorants and fulmar petrels. I've no doubt he watched the seals playing on the sand-banks too." Grandpa smiled at Dan. They both shared a love of the wild life on the island. "All the same, I'll have a word with your Grandma about calling you Dan."

"Don't bother, Grandpa," Dan said suddenly. "Grandma can keep on calling me Aidan, but *you* stick to Dan."

3    DOWN BY THE LIME KILNS

"I wish I'd a radio I could carry around," Dan said next morning at breakfast. "Tom Watson's got one."

"And a right racket he makes with it in the street!" his mother said. "We get enough noise on the island from the tourists' radios. Every car seems to have one going full blast. Silly programmes they are, too, lots of them!"

"Surely you wouldn't be wanting to listen to 'pop' music all the time, like Tom Watson does," Grandma Reid remarked.

"There are other programmes besides pop music," Dan protested. "There are programmes about birds and animals and—and *seals*," he told her.

"You'll just have to save your pocket money if you want a radio transistor, Dan," his mother said. "Next term you go to the school on the mainland and you'll be needing a new outfit then, and football boots and all, and money buys less and less these days."

Dan looked disappointed, but he knew what his mother said was quite true. It only needed a winter of storms to wreck the lobster pots, or the seals to break the salmon nets as they tried to get at the salmon, for his father to have a bad season's fishing and make money scarce. That was why his mother went to work at the mead factory, to make sure of a steady income to help over the bad times.

His mother smiled at him. "Cheer up, Dan! If your father has a good season, maybe it'll stretch to a pocket radio for your birthday next year."

That sounded an awful long time away to Dan, but he returned his mother's smile. Grandpa Reid listened to the discussion but he took no part in it. He knew there was no love lost between Dan and Tom Watson, but he wondered what had sparked off this sudden wish of Dan's to have a transistor radio like Tom Watson's?

"Coming down to Steel End with me, Dan?" he asked. "I could do with some help to stow the lobster pots aboard."

Steel End was where the little quay enclosed the harbour.

"Yes, I'll come," Dan said at once. He liked to lend a hand with the fishing gear and he loved to go aboard the coble. "I wish Dad would let me go out with you to shoot the lobster pots."

"Some day in the holidays he might." The old man looked at the sea, the waves creaming gently against the turf-lined shore. "It's a good calm day for shooting the lobster pots."

"Shooting the pots" was a fisherman's term for casting the pots overboard in the shallow waters off the reefs where the lobsters bred.

The tide was flowing quietly over the sandy flats and advancing towards the causeway which united the island and the mainland. The fog of the previous evening had vanished and the sun cast a gleaming path across the sea. The shining rays reached the Dancing Stone, called by some folk the Riding Stone, a rock in the bay. The waves were beginning to lap up its sides near to the top. When the top was covered by the sea, the folk on that side of the island knew the tide had reached the causeway and that it was no longer possible to cross it to the mainland: Lindisfarne was an island again for another six hours.

Dan worked with a will, helping his grandfather to stack

the lobster pots on the deck as his father handed them up.
The pots were not "pots" at all in the usual sense of the word:
they were like net baskets made of strong rope, fastened
round three hoops of aluminium which were fixed in a
wooden base, over an inch thick. The "pots" or creels had
to be stout to stand the battering they had to take from the
rough seas. Inside the rope basket was a finer netted funnel
which ran inward from the side of the creel. The entrance
was a ring of hazel wood known as the "eye". In most pots
there were two rings and funnels at each end. A flap laced
with twine to a short wooden rod allowed the fishermen to
fix the bait inside the inner net funnel and fasten it to the
bottom of the creel by a double length of twine. Each creel
was weighted by a heavy stone on the wooden base to hold
it in place on the sea-bed.

Already James Reid had baited the pots with strips of
mackerel and decaying fish-heads. He had been up before
breakfast busy at the baiting, working in the old upturned
boat which served him as a store shed. A stout rope was fitted
through a loop at the top of each creel, with a good length
allowed between one creel and the next; several creels being
on the same rope. On the rope between each creel was a cork
float. This was to keep any slack rope from fouling the rocks.
At each end of the rope was a round metal buoy, yellow in
colour. This was the marker buoy which would float on the
surface and tell Peter and James Reid where their lobster
pots lay when they came to lift them. That would not be
till Monday for the lobster boats did not put out to sea on
a Sunday.

Dan carefully arranged the creels neatly in order with the
rope and the cork floats coiled tidily between each one.

"Good work, Dan! We'll make a fisherman of you one
day," his grandfather told him.

"I'd like to be one *now*," Dan said. "I wish I hadn't to

go to that school at Tweedmouth. I'd rather go fishing and earn money."

His father laughed. "What! At nine years old? The time for work'll come all too soon, laddie, and don't think you'll make your fortune at the fishing. Make the most of your schooldays. You'll find you like the school at Tweedmouth when you get there. You may learn something that'll give you the idea of doing a different job from fishing later on. Not but what I'd be glad to have you join me in the 'Jenny' just as I joined Grandpa when I left school."

"That's what I want to do," Dan said stoutly.

"Why are you so keen to earn money?" Grandpa asked with curiosity.

"To buy a transistor radio. That's what I'm saving up my pocket money for," Dan told him, a trifle defiantly.

His grandfather gave him a shrewd look. "You said at breakfast that Tom Watson had got one, didn't you?"

"Yes, and he's always showing off with it and he sneers at me because I haven't got one."

"Neither have lots of other boys," his father reminded him. "There's no need for you to feel inferior to Tom Watson just because he's got something that you haven't."

"No, indeed!" Grandpa agreed. "It's not what people *have* that makes them worth respecting. It's what they *are* and what they can *do*. You remember that, Dan! Come to that, I guess Tom Watson could never make as good a job of stacking lobster pots as you have done just now."

Dan cheered up at once. A word of praise from his grandfather meant a lot to him.

"Just come to the wheel-house with me, Dan, while I look in the pocket of my coat," Grandpa said.

Dan followed him. Often when Dan had done a good job helping with the boat's gear, Grandpa would feel in his coat-pocket and produce a paper bag of treacle caramels or mint drops. Today, however, it was neither of these. From his deep pocket Grandpa brought out something shining. It was a mouth-organ!

"Here you are, Dan! I had that when I was a young man and went out with the herring-boats. It whiled away many a dull evening for all of us, for I could play all the popular tunes then. You learn to play it, laddie! Anyone can switch on a radio but it's not everyone who can play a mouth-organ. You'll be one up on Tom Watson with that." The old man grinned at Dan.

Dan's eyes shone with delight. He took the mouth-organ in his hand as if it was made of gold.

"Go on! Try it!" his father urged him.

Dan put it to his mouth and tried a flourish up and down the scale.

"No' bad!" his grandfather approved.

"You'll soon get the hang of it," his father said. "But, for goodness' sake, do your practising *outside* the house in some quiet place or you'll drive your Grandma silly."

'I'll do that," Dan promised. He was just about to put the instrument to his mouth again when the sound of distant shots came to them over the water.

His father nodded in the direction of the Farne Islands, misty shapes to the south-east. "They're at it again," he remarked. "It will be on all week."

"Aye, the seal-culling's well under way," Grandpa Reid agreed. "Well, no doubt it has to be," he sighed.

"Yes, if we're to have any salmon in our nets," Dan's father added.

On the Farne Islands about seven miles away the grey seals bred in hundreds. They lay close-packed on the rocks and even on the higher ground of the islands. In late October and early November the seal-calves were born, looking like new-born lambs in their white silky fur skins: and now, in the third week of November, the selected seal-killing was allowed by law. Another volley of shots echoed faintly over the sea. Dan listened, his face turned towards the Farne Islands.

"They ... they won't kill the baby seals, will they?" he faltered. He had seen the baby seals and their mothers on the rocks of the Farnes when his father had taken him in the boat, and he had watched them, fascinated. The seals seemed so friendly, raising their heads inquisitively to peer at the boat.

His father answered Dan's question. "No. The Norwegian experts who do the shooting leave the mothers and baby seals alone. They aim at the second- and third-year-old calves and they can only kill a limited number."

"Why do men from Norway come all that way to shoot them?" Dan asked.

His father and grandfather exchanged glances. "The fishermen on this coast aren't keen to kill the seals even if they take the salmon. At Seahouses the fishermen make quite a good thing by taking visitors in their boats to see the seals on the Farnes," Peter Reid told Dan.

"There's a strange thing too," Grandpa added. "The seals make moaning sounds, almost a queer kind of singing. In foggy weather the sound carries a long way and it warns fishermen when their boats are too close to the Farnes. Maybe boats have been saved from shipwreck by the seals singing."

"Aye, but salmon fishermen have lost their living too because of the seals breaking the nets and biting the salmon in them," Peter Reid pointed out. "Well, Dad, if we are going to make *our* living today with a lobster catch we'd better push off now." He started the small diesel engine and Grandpa Reid took over the wheel.

"So long, Dan!" he called as Dan scrambled on to the stone pier. "Now don't go and torture your grandmother's ears with that mouth organ or *I'll* get a row when we come back!"

The "Jenny" began to move slowly out from the jetty. Dan watched them steer into the middle of the harbour, gave

them a wave, then turned and ran along the pier to the grass-edged beach. He took out his mouth-organ and looked at it with delight, gave a quick flourish up the scale, then thrust it back in his pocket again. He had his usual Saturday morning jobs to do for his mother and Grandmother. There was the milk to fetch from St Coomb's farm, the potatoes to peel for dinner, shoes to clean for Sunday's church-going and maybe errands to run too. There would be no time to practise on his mouth-organ till after the midday dinner.

As soon as dinner was over Dan snatched up his anorak and made for the door.

"You're in a mighty hurry," Kate told him. "What's on in the village?"

"N-nothing," Dan said. "Nothing I know of." He was in two minds whether to show Kate his mouth-organ, but he decided he would learn to play it first and then surprise her. He didn't want her to laugh because he produced weird noises with it.

"I'm just off to look at some sea-birds along the shore. I'll be back soon," he called over his shoulder as he slammed the door behind him.

"That lad's crazy about birds," his mother said. "He does know an awful lot about the different kinds that come to the island. I think that's one of the reasons why he doesn't want to go to school on the mainland. I wish he'd get round to liking the idea, though, for he'll have to go there next term. You like it, don't you, Kate?"

"Oh, yes!" Kate said at once. "We learn all kinds of new things, like gymnastics and cookery."

"I canna' see Aidan being over-enthusiastic about cookery," Grandma remarked with a slight sniff.

"Oh, but the boys play football too, you know, and there aren't enough boys on the island for a football team, Grandma."

"Och, there's a deal too much made of football these days!" Grandma Reid turned down the corners of her mouth. "Nothing but football in the papers and on the telly! I get fair sick of it. Maybe I'm just an old body but I reckon there are other things in life besides football. Aidan's all right as he is."

"Let's get the dishes tidied away and then we can get our

knitting out and put our feet up," Mrs Reid said tactfully
to avoid further argument. "It won't be long before the
men are back from the boat and they'll be wanting their
teas."

Meanwhile Dan had reached the shore. At first he thought
of going into the family's shed, made of the old up-turned
coble's hulk, but at a nearby shed two fishermen were mend-
ing their salmon nets. Dan did not want an audience for his
first attempts on the mouth-organ. It would not be long
before the November dusk fell, so it was too late to cross the
island to lonely Sandon Bay. He had a sudden bright idea.
He would go to Castle Point, to the old lime kilns that nestled
under the cliffs below Beblowe Castle. No one would be there
on a chilly November Saturday: and he could even go into
one of the old kilns like a cave at the water's edge and be
out of everyone's sight. It would be fun to hear what echoes
his mouth-organ raised in the hollow kilns.

The tide was still up but beginning to ebb. It was too close
in to the rocks yet for Dan to get round by the shore path,
but he could take the cliff path that wound round the foot
of the castle hill, and then descend by the grassy track to
the old waggon way that led to the lime kilns.

Dan reached the high wall that guarded the brick shafts
down into the lime kilns. Down these shafts long ago, the
lime burners had poured their coal. At one point there was
a stile over the wall, but a notice beside it warned people
that it was dangerous to allow children or dogs to cross the
wall because of the open shafts. Dan mounted the stile and
took his customary peep over the wall. The great brick shafts
yawned below him, echoing the wash of the tide at the entrance to the kilns on the beach below. Dan thought he
caught the flash and flutter of wings near the seaward edge
of the lime kilns. He watched a couple of guillemots swooping
and diving for fish out in the bay—most likely they had a

Castle Crag

Upper Path

To Old Waggon Way

Wall        Steps        Wall

Kilns

Vents

Steep Climb

Steep Climb

Fulmar Petrels Nest

large Kiln

To Lindisfarne Town

Shore Path

Beach

Sea and Sand Flats

The Ouse

Long Rig Sandbank

nest somewhere on the high point of the castle cliff. But the flash of wings he had seen did not belong to the brown-backed guillemots. The brief glimpse he had caught was of a grey back and wings and a white head in a graceful gliding flight. He climbed down from the wall to descend the grassy path and look at the lime kilns from the shore.

Once the lime kilns had been a busy place. Limestone from the quarries in the north of the island had been brought along the old waggon way, now overgrown with weeds, to the kilns at the south-eastern point of the island. There the limestone was burned and loaded into boats at the little wooden jetty close by and taken to the mainland in coastal freighters. Now the kilns were deserted and crumbling. The wooden jetty had been hacked to pieces in fierce storms and only a few posts remained of it, and no sea-going ships tied up there now. Nearly eighty years ago the fires had died out in the kilns and fishermen no longer saw the warning glow that warned them they were near to the treacherous sand-banks of Long Rig.

Dan took the steep path down by the side of the kilns. At its foot were the openings to three tunnels leading deep into the kilns below the deep shafts. Dan took a quick look inside them, then turned the corner of the cliffs to the front of the kilns facing the shore. Here there were four arches penetrating right into the kilns which rose to an imposing height.

Dan had the whole place to himself and he gave a skirl on his mouth-organ. Suddenly there was an indignant squawk, a fluttering of wings, and two birds, something like large seagulls, rose in the air. Dan stared at them. He said to himself, "But those birds aren't gulls. Their backs and wings are too dark grey." He stood quietly till the birds settled down again on a grass-grown ledge just at the top corner of the kilns. There they had made a shallow nest lined with dry grass and tufts of sea-pinks. Dan watched them closely and the birds watched Dan.

"They've not got a red spot on their beaks like herring-gulls," he noted. "They've got peculiar beaks, too, with kind of tubes in them, like nostrils." He thought over the pictures he had seen in Grandpa's bird books and all at once he gave a sharp "Oh!" which made the birds poke up their heads and look at him suspiciously again with their beady eyes. "I know!" he said. "They're fulmar petrels!"

His eyes shone with delight. Though the fulmar petrels bred on the Farne Islands, he had never seen any on Lindisfarne before. Now they had chosen to nest at Castle Point. That would be something to tell his grandfather—but no one else, certainly none of his school mates, for fear they might come and disturb the birds.

"I'll go inside the lime kilns and play my mouth-organ so I don't disturb the petrels," he decided, and took himself under the largest pointed arch, higher than the other three arches and well away from the birds' nest.

It was very dark inside the cave-like hollow of the kiln. Dan went a short way in, sat down on a fallen stone and pulled out his mouth-organ. He tried a scale or two up and down it, then one or two notes to find where they were on the mouth-piece. After a couple of mistakes he was beginning to find the right notes fairly well. "I'll try a tune now," he said to himself. "What shall I try? It had better be an easy one, something with a good beat to it, like a hymn."

He broke into *Onward Christian soldiers, marching as to war!* and managed the first two lines quite successfully. The third line, however, ended in a bit of a screech.

"I'll try again," he said, and repeated the first two lines. This time he was more successful and struggled through to the chorus in a fairly recognisable tune. He was repeating the hymn for the third time when he heard a sound, a cross between a moan and a bleating whine. It seemed to come from further inside the kiln. Dan froze into stillness, but no further sound came.

"It must have been an echo," he said to himself. Once more he put the mouth-organ to his lips.

He had hardly got through the first line of his tune when the moaning sound came again. From the recess of the kiln came a slight stirring. Dan felt fear rise in his throat. For a moment he felt like rushing out into the daylight and taking to his heels, but he was no coward.

"Who's there?" he called in a shaky voice.

There was no reply, only another slight sound like a body stirring on gravel.

Dan had the sudden thought that someone might have fallen down one of the bricked shafts above into the kiln below, a visitor to the island, perhaps, who had not been aware of the dangers and had gone exploring among the un-fenced shafts? He might be lying there only partly conscious. Dan felt in his anorak pocket for his other prized possession, his pocket torch. He snatched it out and shone it into the depths of the kiln. From a few feet away two large luminous eyes stared at him. Dan gave a terrified shudder but he stood his ground.

The eyes did not move. They came no closer. Behind them Dan could see a humped-up shape lying on the ground. He ventured a little nearer. The light from his torch fell on a dog-like face and a white shiny fur-like skin.

Dan gave a gasp. "It's a seal!" He went nearer still, but not near enough for the seal to snap at him. In his relief at finding nothing horrible he put his mouth-organ to his lips and sounded a chord. From the seal there came a reply, a singing kind of wail!

"Jings!" he exclaimed. "Grandma said that seals could *sing*. I've found a singing seal!"

He ventured within an arm's length of the seal, keeping his torch focused on it.

"It's a very small seal," he said to himself. "It's got a white coat so it must be still a baby, only two or three weeks old. I wonder how it got here?" He shone his torch round the kiln, but there was no sign of the mother seal. "It seemed to reply to my playing. Perhaps I sounded like another seal."

Dan laughed at himself. Once more he put the instrument to his mouth and played a bar of his tune. The seal responded in a wavering kind of whine.

"I do believe you're trying to talk to me," Dan said, and came within a foot of the small seal. It did not shrink away nor try to snap at him, but thrust its head forward and looked at him with large melting eyes. Dan took a deep breath and bent over it and gently stroked the hump of its spine. The seal turned its head but made no attempt to bite. It seemed to like being stroked.

"I wonder if your mother will come back to find you?" Dan asked aloud. "Maybe she's just gone off swimming to catch a fish or two, but she'll surely come back to feed you?"

Dan looked out over the water. The guns were silent now on the Farne Islands. Already the evening dusk was closing in and a mist was beginning to shroud the island.

"I'll have to go now, little seal," Dan said in a crooning voice, giving the seal a last gentle stroke along its back. "But I'll come back to see you tomorrow though I expect your mother will have come and taken you away by then."

He gave a last clash of chords on his mouth-organ and the seal joined in with its quavering wailing note, then Dan thrust the mouth-organ into his pocket and went out, turning back up the cliff path.

"Fulmar petrels *and* a baby seal! Jings! What a stroke of luck! Some time I'll tell Grandpa about the fulmar petrels, but I think I won't tell anyone about the seal, not yet. Anyway, by tomorrow its mother may have taken it back to wherever it came from."

Dan hurried home to the cottage where already Grandma was busy getting the tea ready.

# 4 PROBLEMS FOR DAN

The next day Dan slipped out of the cottage as soon as it was light enough to see the path by the cliff. No one was stirring yet, but once breakfast was over Dan knew he would have no chance to go along to the lime kilns before church. In the afternoon they would be going to have tea with Aunt Meg in Fenkle Street. So it was now or never, if he was to see whether the seal had vanished in the night.

By the time Dan had reached the kilns the sun had risen and was shining directly on the east side of the kiln. The fulmar petrels at the other end lifted their heads, stood up and gave a squawk or two as he approached the big arched entrance, but they did not even bother to flutter out of the nest. Dan gave a cheeky skirl on his mouth-organ at them; then, just inside the kiln, he played the first two lines of his hymn. A low bleating wail answered him. The seal was still there.

Dan switched on his torch and advanced a step or two nearer, still playing his mouth-organ. The little seal answered in a quavering moan. To Dan's quick ear the seal's reply sounded more feeble than on the previous afternoon. He went nearer and switched on his torch. The seal's beautiful eyes looked at him in mute appeal. When he stroked its back there was an answering quiver and the seal made a slight whimpering sound. Dan looked about on the floor of the lime kiln and along the stretch of beach below it but there were no marks of any heavy body having dragged itself over the shingle. The fulmar petrels watched suspiciously from their nest. Dan went back to the seal and sat on the big stone beside it and brought out his mouth-organ again. This time he tried other tunes that were simple and easy to play. He tried a Scottish lullaby that Grandma used to sing when he and Kate were small:

> *Eeh-oh, eeh-oh, what shall I do wi' thee?*
> *Eeh-oh, eeh-oh, nothing for to give thee,*
> *Black's the life that I lead wi' thee.*

The little seal joined in, uttering a quavering sound as though it was trying to sing, but at the end it panted and gave a sad little whine. Dan looked at the seal pityingly. "I think you must be hungry," he said. "Why don't you try to get into the sea and catch fish?" He ventured to stroke it as he had done before. The seal did not show any fear but seemed to find comfort in the touch of Dan's hand.

"Come on then," Dan said, taking a step or two towards the entrance to the kiln. The seal put out a flipper as though it would like to follow him and edged a little forward, then collapsed as though exhausted.

"You're just weak with hunger," Dan said. "Hold on a bit and I'll try to find you a fish."

He hurried back round the point to the curve of the bay. Sometimes the fishermen left small fish in their sheds to use as bait for their lobster pots. On Sunday morning no one was at the sheds, but Dan knew where his father kept the key, in a little hollow under the boat-shed. He unlocked the door and looked in. He was in luck. A small mackerel lay under the bench. Dan locked the shed again and sprinted back over the rough track by the castle and down to the shore. The fulmar petrels gave excited squawks when they

saw the fish he was carrying, but Dan charged straight on
into the lime kiln. He held out the fish to the seal but the
seal just gave a sniff and made no attempt to take it from
him.

"Come on! Eat it!" Dan urged the seal, putting the fish
close to its mouth. Again the seal sniffed at it, but then turned
its head away. Dan tried again, even wiping the seal's
whiskers with the dead fish, but the seal lowered its head
and would not open its mouth. Tears gathered in its large
eyes and rolled down its face.

"Good gracious! It's crying like a baby! After all, it *is* a
baby. Maybe baby seals don't eat fish?"

Dan tried again to persuade the seal to take the fish, but again it showed no interest in it.

"It's no use!" Dan cried. In frustration he flung the mackerel out on to the shingle. There were some excited cries and the fulmar petrels swooped down upon it; each seized hold of the fish and there was a tug of war. The fish was soon pulled to pieces and gobbled up.

"Well, they like it, even if you don't." Dan gave the seal a gentle pat on its back. "I wouldn't like them to get at you," he went on. Dan guessed the fulmar petrels would not attack the seal until they thought it was too weak to resist them, but if it didn't get food it would soon grow weaker. Somehow he must find out what baby seals ate and bring food along. Perhaps Grandpa might know? He was wise about the ways of all sea-creatures.

By now the day had grown quite light and Dan knew he must get back home before he was late for breakfast. "I've got to go now," he told the little seal, giving it a final stroke. "But I'll be back."

Almost as if imploring him to stay, the seal gave a whimper like a baby crying when Dan turned away.

"Where can its mother be?" Dan wondered, full of pity. "Seals usually take great care of their babies." He remembered seeing the cow-seals on the Farnes putting their bodies between their seal-pups and the sightseers in boats. He had seen the seals, too, stroking their babies affectionately with their flippers, and once he had even seen a cow-seal giving her young one a first swimming lesson, pushing it gently along with her chest towards a shallow gunnel between rocks so it was not carried out to sea by the drag of the tide. Seal-pups soon learned to swim, even when only a few days old, and this small seal must have been able to swim some distance to have reached the lime kilns, Dan reasoned. But why had the mother abandoned her seal-pup?

The family was up and about when he reached the cottage. Grandma was giving a stir to the porridge pot and Grandpa had already taken his seat at the table.

"My! You've been out early," he said to Dan.

"I went to practise on my mouth-organ by the lime kilns," Dan told him. "And, Grandpa, I saw some strange sea-birds."

"What! Birds again!" Kate gave an affectionate rumple to Dan's hair as she passed to take her seat at the table.

"What kind of birds?" Grandpa asked.

"Grandpa, I *think* they're fulmar petrels. They're like the picture in your bird book."

Grandpa was interested at once. "Those birds mostly stay on the Farnes. It's not often they nest here. What were the birds like?"

"Darkish grey backs with white head and breasts, yellow legs, but their beaks were funny. They were shorter and broader than a herring-gull's and they had two peculiar tubes like nostrils."

"Well observed, Dan!" Grandpa nodded approval. "They do indeed sound like fulmar petrels, and though they don't often nest on Lindisfarne, they've been known to do so. But the bit you describe about their beaks seems to clinch it, they *are* fulmars. Don't you go too near them, though, or you'll find out what they use those tube-like nostrils for." Grandpa laughed.

"What for, Grandpa?"

"A rather nasty dirty habit that fulmars have if people go too near their nests. They vomit up what's in their stomachs and blow it through their nostrils at their attackers. What they spit out smells horrible, as they like oily fish to eat."

"Oh, don't, Grandpa! You'll spoil my breakfast! What filthy birds!" Kate cried.

"It's just their way of defending themselves, Kate, and really you can't blame them if they think their nests are going to be attacked."

"Stop chattering and get on with your breakfasts, all of you, if you don't want to be late for church. There are still the dishes to wash and put by," Grandma reminded them sharply.

Grandpa gave a sideways wink at Dan. "I'll come and have a look at those birds some day, laddie, when I've got a bit of time to spare."

Later, when Dan was helping his grandfather to stack the dishes on a tray he took the opportunity to ask quietly, "What do baby seals feed on, Grandpa?"

"Why, laddie, the seal-mother's milk, just as calves get milk from cows."

"But don't they eat fish? I thought all seals ate fish."

"Not when they're very young, any more than you would expect human babies to eat steak and chips when they're a few days old. Seals grow very fast, though, and by the end of three weeks they could be three times the weight they are when they're born. That's when their mothers begin to wean them and to teach them to catch fish."

"Is it ordinary milk, like cow's milk, that they get, to make them grow so fast?" Dan asked.

"Oh, no! It's a lot richer than cow's milk, very creamy, more like condensed milk or tinned cream, I'd think," Grandpa told him. He gave Dan a quick curious glance. "What makes you ask, Dan?"

"Oh, I just wondered..." Dan said vaguely, unwilling to tell his secret yet. He was saved from further questioning by Grandma's voice coming from the back-kitchen. "Hurry up with that tray, you two! I'm standing waiting for the rest of the dishes."

"Have you cleaned your shoes again, Dan?" his mother

called. "They'll be muddy after you've been on the shore and I won't have you turning up with dirty shoes in church."

Dan hastened to get out the shoe-brushes. As he brushed his shoes, he thought of what his grandfather had said. So, if he wanted to keep the seal alive he would have to get condensed milk.

Dan glanced rapidly over the store-cupboard. The Reids got fresh milk daily from St Coomb's farm, so it was not likely there would be any condensed milk on the shelves. But then Dan suddenly remembered that his grandmother sometimes made 'tablet', a sweet sugary fudge toffee, and for that she used a tin of condensed milk. He looked hurriedly behind the foremost tins. Sure enough, there was a tin of condensed milk.

Dan hesitated. The shop in the Square did not open on Sunday, and it opened just too late in the morning for Dan to buy a tin himself and get along to the shore with it and give it to the seal before school. In any case, he didn't want to take the tin to school with him and have other boys ask him silly questions. Perhaps he could just *borrow* the tin on the shelf and replace it tomorrow? In his money-box in his bedroom he had the money that he had been saving up for a transistor radio, but after all, now he had the mouth-organ the transistor didn't seem as important. He could easily buy three or four tins of condensed milk with the money he had. Grandma would hardly be likely to be making 'tablet' on Monday which was washing-day, and by midday he would have replaced the tin on the shelf. It would just be *borrowing* the tin for a day, so he could keep the seal-calf alive.

Dan knew he ought to ask his mother or his grandmother first if he might have the tin, but they would be sure to ask what he wanted it for and that would mean telling them about the seal, and then, maybe, they would say "No! It's just a piece of nonsense." And then there might be no chance of saving the baby seal's life. He decided to borrow the tin when no one was in the back-kitchen and to pay it back next day.

"My! you're taking a long time to clean those shoes, Dan," his mother said, looking round the door to find Dan with the brush poised in his hand and a faraway look in his eyes.

"Aidan'll be in a dwawm about those birds," Grandma chuckled. "Dwawm" was Grandma's Scottish word that meant a condition between sleeping and waking.

"No, Grandma! It's about seals this time." The words were out of Dan's mouth before he realised what he had said. Grandma just laughed, but in the living-room Grandpa heard Dan's reply and paused as he filled up his pipe.

"Now, what has the lad got in his head about seals? There's *something* bothering him and it's more than just Grandma's old tales, I'm thinking."

What with everyone coming and going in the living-room and back-kitchen on Sunday, and then going to church, followed by dinner, and then Grandpa having a nap in the armchair while young Mrs Reid read a book, and Kate sat at the table making a map for her homework, there was no chance for Dan to take away the tin.

"I'll have to get it during the night when everyone is asleep," Dan decided.

"Dan, for goodness' sake, stop wandering round like a lost soul and get a book and read till it's time to go to Aunt Meg's," his mother said.

The afternoon seemed to loiter along for Dan. Aunt Meg got out the Scrabble game for him and Kate, but Dan's mind was not on the game.

"Hi, Dan! You don't spell 'guess' like 'geuss', you goose!" Kate told him. "You'll have to spell better than that when you come to the mainland school. I thought you were a good speller."

Two moves further on Dan put down the letters for "seal" when he meant to put "sole".

"You can't *do* that!" Kate said in exasperation. "You've got to have a word that ends in an 'e'. A grand fisherman you'll make if you can't tell a sole from a seal!"

Grandpa looked sharply across the room at Dan, but Dan did not reply to Kate. The word "seal" had also attracted his father's attention.

"I was having a word with Sam Cromarty as we came out of church and he was telling me that a dead seal had been washed up on the Long Rig Bank and left there at low tide yesterday," Peter Reid told his father. Dan looked up quickly and listened.

"It was a cow-seal," his father went on. "She seemed to have been shot. She could have come from the Farnes—but the Norwegian marksmen are pretty good and they don't shoot the cow-seals."

"Aye, they're careful, I'll grant them that," Grandpa said. "Maybe she took fright at the shooting and was killed accidentally as she swam away from the islands. Perhaps she was protecting a pup."

Dan pricked up his ears.

"No sign of any pup on the Long Rig bank. If there *was* a pup it could have been washed ashore somewhere else along the coast. The seal-cullers do sometimes have difficulty in getting the bodies of the seals they shoot."

"I wish they didn't have to cull the seals, though I know it's necessary," Grandma said.

Dan gave her a warm loving look which his grandfather did not miss.

"You should see the hole a seal made in my salmon net a while ago and the great pieces bitten out of the salmon's back," Peter Reid told her.

The talk drifted to the price of nylon nets and the market

price of fish. Dan forgot about his game and stared through the window. So that was what had happened to the baby seal's mother, he thought. The high tide must have washed the pup ashore right into the very entrance to the lime kilns. The little seal must have crawled in there, terrified, waiting for its mother to rescue it. A surge of pity swept over Dan.

"Come on! It's your turn to play," Kate reminded him.

With an effort Dan came back to the game.

At last it was time to go home. It was quite dark as they trudged along Fenkle Street and by St Cuthbert's Square, and it was near bedtime when they got home.

"We'd better all have an early bed tonight. We've got to be up in good time so Kate can get the school bus tomorrow. It'll be an early start to get away before the tide comes up," young Mrs Reid said.

"Don't forget that I'll be home earlier than usual next Friday," Kate reminded them. "It's our half-term holiday next week-end."

"It'll be our half-term holiday too," Dan said.

"Oh, good!" Kate replied. "We'll do something special, shall we?"

Dan nodded and looked thoughtful. Perhaps at half-term he could tell Kate about the seal if it was still there?

"Bedtime now," their mother said firmly.

Dan slept in the attic at the top of the house up a steep wooden stair. As he went up he tested each stair carefully to find out which one creaked. It was the fourth from the top. Dan dropped his white handkerchief on it so he would see it in the gloom. He did not quite close the door of his bedroom but left it ajar. That made sure there would be no rattle of the handle. He leaned out of his dormer window and watched the white line of the waves as they curled lazily over the beach in the moonlight. Across the bay he thought he could just make out the dim outline of the lime kilns where his seal would be.

"I'll be coming to you tomorrow," he whispered into the darkness.

Dan listened to the quiet rumble of the grown-up voices in the living-room. It seemed a long time before he heard his parents come up the stairs to bed and the door close on the landing below. Even then it was an hour before he dared venture down the stairs. At last, feeling like a thief in the night, he stood on the top step and switched on his flash-light, keeping the beam low. Then, slowly, step by step, hesitating on each one and listening for sounds from his parents' bedroom, he made his way down. Grasping the hand-rail he made a long stride over the creaky stair and at last he reached the foot of the wooden staircase. Now he had to tackle the longer flight to the ground floor. It seemed to take him hours before he reached the closed door of the living-room. There he had to be doubly careful, for his grandfather and grandmother slept in the "bed-closet", a recess in the living-room like that in many another northern house. It was curtained off from the rest of the room in the daytime; at night, though, the curtains were drawn back to reveal a bed. This gave extra sleeping space to many a family. Grandma Reid said she liked sleeping there: "It's fine and warm of a winter's night beside the fire," she would declare.

"Aye, and it's right handy for me to bring you a cup of tea in the morning, Mary, without having to mount all those stairs," Grandpa Reid agreed.

Dan just hoped that Grandma Reid was not longing for a cup of tea in the middle of the night!

The back-kitchen was just on the other side of the passage. Dan grasped the door handle and turned it very gently. Another moment and he was inside the room. He opened the store-cupboard softly and flashed his light along the shelves. The tin of condensed milk was there at the back of the other tins and packets. It was just beyond the reach of his hand.

"Bother! I'll have to stand on a chair," Dan breathed.

Carefully he lifted a wooden chair and set it down quietly beside the cupboard. Even then he waited a minute and listened before he climbed on to it. Then he reached out for the tin. Another moment and it was in his hand and he had stuffed it up the front of his jersey. Just as he was stepping down from the chair his elbow caught an enamel jug and sent it flying. It fell with a loud clatter on the stone floor. Someone *must* be wakened by it! Quick as thought, Dan jumped down from the chair, turned on a tap in the nearby sink and lifted a cup from the hook. He heard his grandfather say something, then get out of bed; and the living-room door was opened.

"Who's there?" his grandfather called.

"Just me, Dan!" Dan's voice trembled slightly.

The light was switched on. "What are you doing there?" his grandfather demanded.

"Just getting a drink," Dan told him quite truthfully. "I— I'm sorry I knocked the jug down and wakened you."

"Off up the stairs with you then, quietly, and don't wake anyone else," his grandfather told him sternly.

Dan set down the cup and vanished up the stairs like a dark ghost.

"What was it, James?" Grandma Reid asked sleepily when Grandpa returned to bed.

"Just Dan getting a drink," Grandpa told her. "He hadn't switched on the light and he knocked the enamel jug down."

It was not till he got into bed that he realised that Dan was not dressed in his pyjamas. "Now, what was the laddie up to?" he asked himself puzzled.

Shivering, Dan flung off his clothes and climbed into bed,

but first he stuffed the tin into the pocket of his jeans. Tomorrow he would conceal it in his school bag. He felt guilty, like a thief. Sleep did not come easily.

"Tomorrow I'll get another tin at the shop and put it in the cupboard," he promised himself. "I've not really *stolen* it, just borrowed it."

At last he fell asleep, a sleep that was haunted by the pitiful crying of a baby seal and the cries of sea-birds.

TOM WATSON GETS SUSPICIOUS

Although he had missed a great deal of his night's sleep Dan was up early next morning. He found his grandmother already setting the table for breakfast and his grandfather raking the fire.

"My, lad, you're early!" Grandma greeted him. "What's got into you?"

"I'm away to the farm to get the milk," Dan told her.

"I've got enough for breakfast. They'll hardly have begun milking the cows by now."

"It doesn't matter. I can wait till they've done," Dan said desperately, seizing the milk can. He fled out of the door before she could ask any more questions.

The puzzled look came into his grandfather's face. He went to the window and watched Dan running along the road by the beach. "He's not taking the cross-road to the farm. He's making for the shore round the Ouse. What's he want there?"

"Some ploy of his own," Grandma remarked. "Maybe he's after bait for his fishing."

Grandpa Reid watched the small figure make its way to the rocky foreshore and follow the slippery path over the rocks. "Why! He's heading towards Castle Point!"

"Didn't he tell you about some birds he saw there yesterday? Fulmar petrels, weren't they? Maybe he's gone to take a look at them?" Grandma suggested. "Right daft about birds, that laddie is!"

"Maybe you're right, but he'd be wiser to keep his distance from the petrels if they've got young ones."

"Och! Aidan's got plenty of sense. He's too fond of the birds to go annoying them."

"True! But perhaps I'll go take a look at those birds myself sometime," Grandpa replied. "It can't be today, though. We've got the lobster pots to lift and the lobsters to crate ready for the van to take them to Berwick."

Sure-footed, Dan went along the rocky sea-weeded path round the Ouse towards the lime kilns. In one pocket of his jeans was the condensed milk; in the other, the tin-opener, which Dan had snatched from the rack on his way out. The mouth-organ was in the pocket beside it. The sky was a pale yellow in the east behind Beblowe Hill where a watery sun

was rising over the North Sea. On the sand-flats the wader birds were already feeding at the edge of the tide. The eider ducks, known on Lindisfarne as "St Cuthbert's ducks", were darting hither and thither in the shallow water. The sand-pipers were rising in rapid flight from their nests in the long grass beyond the castle, uttering their mournful shrill cries as they flew to their feeding-grounds on the sand-banks. The oyster-catchers with their long coral-red bills were already on the hunt for mussels and limpets among the rocks, making short uneasy flights, paddling restlessly up and down on the shore, calling to each other in a shrill rattling whistle. Dan knew and loved them all, and another time he would have been tempted to stay and watch them, but not today. Today he must hasten to his seal.

He reached the lime kilns. The fulmar petrels in their nest at the top of the western-most kiln rose in fluttering annoyance, giving their shrill squawks of indignation, but when Dan passed their corner eyrie and did not come near them, they settled down once more.

Dan approached the kiln entrance and pulled out his mouth-organ. He took a deep breath. Suppose there was no answer to his music? What if the little seal had already died of hunger? He sounded the first trembling notes of *The Blue-bells of Scotland*. When he reached the second bar there came a moaning wavering sound from inside the kiln. Dan's heart gave a throb of joy. The seal was alive and, what was more, had recognised his signal and replied to it. Dan pulled the tin of condensed milk from his pocket and hurried into the kiln, still playing his mouth-organ. The seal looked up at him with limpid eyes. Dan spoke to it quietly and caressingly. "Still alone? You poor little creature. I'll guess you're hungry."

He gave the seal a gentle little pat. The seal quivered at his touch and tried weakly to raise a flipper as if to touch

Dan in turn, then feebly flopped back again. Dan set to work to open the tin of milk.

"You'll like this," he said.

The seal watched him with the curiosity of all seals but made no effort to move. Dan got the tin open, then he looked at the jagged edge in dismay. "I can't give it to you in *this*! You'd cut yourself."

Dan looked around in desperation for some kind of utensil from which the seal could lick the milk. Then, all at once, his eyes spied one of the large saucer-like scallop shells that are found on the Northumbrian shores. At the souvenir shop in the mead factory they were sold in half-dozens to tourists who used them to serve shellfish at their dinner tables.

Dan seized this one thankfully, rinsed it in a rock pool and carried it back to the kiln. Then, slowly and carefully, he tipped a few drops of milk into the shell. It would only hold about a tablespoonful.

"We'll try this first," he said, and held the big shell close to the seal's mouth.

The seal drew back slightly, wrinkling its head into the folds of its skin.

"Come on! Take a lick," Dan urged it.

The seal still held back.

"Don't be afraid."

Still the little seal backed its head away.

"Oh, do open your mouth!" Dan begged. "You'll like it."

The seal turned its head sideways and Dan felt utterly frustrated. He ran round to the other side of the seal, but once again the seal turned its head in the opposite direction.

Dan began to feel cross. "Oh, you stupid little thing! Can't you see I'm trying to help you?" He tried to forestall the turn of the head by thrusting the scallop shell on the opposite side, away from him. The seal's nose collided with the shell and half the condensed milk was spilt on the seal's face and whiskers.

"Now look what you've done!" Dan cried.

The seal felt the sticky stuff on its whiskers and nose and instinctively its tongue came out to lick it away. It gave one lick and then another and another. There was almost a look of surprise in its eyes. It watched Dan and the scallop shell he still held in his hand with a flickering interest.

"So, that's what I've to do, is it?" Dan asked. He tipped the shell once again over the seal's nose and whiskers. Again the tongue came out busily, licking and licking.

"You're just a messy little baby!" Dan chuckled as he poured more condensed milk from the tin into the shell. "It's a sticky way of feeding you, but at least you're getting something. It's going to take a long time, though."

Dan was right. He had to be very patient, trickling the milk over the seal's mouth and whiskers. A lot of it ran off the seal's face into the sandy floor of the kiln. Dan tried offering the scallop shell again to the seal, but it backed its head again in refusal.

"What am I to do?" Dan cried. "At this rate I'm going to have to go to school without my breakfast myself and there's still the milk to fetch from the farm."

Again he trickled the milk from the scallop shell and again the seal licked its whiskers clean. Dan was getting desperate. He put the scallop shell to the seal's mouth with a sudden movement and pushed the seal's nose on to it, splashing the milk around. Instinctively the seal's tongue came out again and the scallop shell received a lick too. Dan repeated the move, but this time he pushed the seal's nose more gently into the scallop shell, and the tongue came out and licked not only the whiskers but the scallop shell twice.

"We're getting somewhere at last," Dan sighed. "But it's terrible slow!"

The next try produced the same result. The little seal's face was white and sticky with the condensed milk. Then Dan tried just putting the scallop shell to the seal's mouth without smearing its nose. The seal kept its mouth closed but it did not back away from the shell. Dan patiently held it to the seal's lips. Then perhaps the sweet smell of the milk stimulated the seal. The lips parted and the tongue came out and the seal gave several laps at the milk in the shell.

Dan was delighted. His patience had triumphed. He tried the experiment again and, after the first hesitation, the seal again lapped at the milk.

Dan looked anxiously at his wrist watch, his last birthday present. It was already after eight o'clock and his grandmother would be wondering where he was. He looked at the tin of condensed milk. It was still half-full.

"I'll have to go now, little seal," he said, giving the seal's shoulder a friendly pat. "But I'll come after school and get the rest into you."

He put the half-empty tin under a stone and placed another flat stone on top of it, then sped for all he was worth up the hill to the pathway down from the castle, along the half-mile past the Popple Well, right at the Iron Rails Inn, and along the Straight Loaning to St Coomb's Farm.

The farmer's wife filled his can for him. "My! You're late today, Dan. Did you oversleep?" she laughed.

"No. I had something to do first," Dan called over his shoulder as he ran down the lane.

He burst into the house. "Here's the milk, Grandma!"

"And high time too! Where have you been, Aidan?"

Dan hardly knew what to say. "Er—er—down by the shore."

His grandfather hazarded a guess. "Well, did you see the fulmar petrels? I saw you running towards the lime kilns."

Dan nodded. He *had* seen the fulmar petrels, truthfully, but still he kept silence about the seal.

His grandmother scolded him. "You're just crazy about birds. Had you forgotten breakfast was early to let Kate get off on the mini-bus to the school at Tweedmouth? And now she's gone without a word from you. And your mother's off to her work too."

Dan looked crestfallen. He was fond of Kate and usually he saw her off on the mini-bus if its departure did not interfere with his own time of assembly at school.

"I . . . I'm sorry about that." He almost choked on the words.

"Ah, well, she'll be back a bit earlier this week," his grandfather reminded him, feeling some sympathy with Dan.

Dan felt slightly more cheerful. "I'm sorry I was late with the milk, Grandma."

"It was lucky I still had some in a jug in the pantry," she remarked. "Otherwise I would have had to get out yon condensed stuff. I was just looking for it but I couldna' lay my hands on the tin. And just then you did come in with the milk."

Dan felt a horrid guilty shock. How lucky that he had come in with the milk just at the right moment! But supposing he had not? That tin of condensed milk must be replaced as soon as he could do it.

"Get your porridge now," his Grandma said and passed the bowl to him. Dan covered the porridge with milk to cool it, then, still hot as it was, he swallowed it as quickly as he could.

"Steady on, Dan! Don't choke yourself!" Grandpa warned him. "Well, I'll away to Steel End to join Peter. He'll be wanting to go to the lobster pots as soon as the tide's high enough."

"Time you were off to school too, Aidan," Grandma Reid said with a glance at the "wag-at-the-wall" clock.

Dan scurried upstairs. He seized his money box. He would need money to replace the tin of condensed milk. He scrabbled in his drawer for the key and couldn't find it. Surely he had put it under that pile of socks? In desperation he tipped the contents of the drawer on his unmade bed. The key slipped out and fell between the bed and the wall. Frantically Dan crept under the bed and scraped round with his hands in the shadows till he found it. Another moment and he had his money box open.

"How much is condensed milk?" Dan wondered. "Oh, I'd better take the lot and be sure." Luckily his money box was fairly full as he had been saving his pocket money. He stuffed the money into his pocket. "I'll need *two* tins, one to put back and one for the seal."

His grandmother's voice came from down below. "What *are* you doing, Aidan? Hurry up, or you'll be late for school."

Dan snatched up the contents of the drawer and stuffed them into it, putting the drawer back with a slam and leaving half a jersey sleeve hanging out.

"Are you coming, Aidan?" his grandmother called impatiently.

"Just getting my school books!" Dan called back, as he grabbed his school bag and clattered down the stairs. Before his grandmother could say any more he had banged the door behind him and was away like the wind round the corner and into St Cuthbert's Square, taking the short cut to the school.

Dan's mind was not on his schoolwork that morning. Twice he had to be called to attention by the teacher for dreaming. All the time he was thinking of ways and means to feed his seal. How much would tins of condensed milk cost? Was there enough money in his pocket from his money box? He fingered the coins in his pocket and tried to count them by the feel of his fingers, but it was not easy. Tom Watson sat next to him and he heard the clink of coins in Dan's pocket and was curious.

"What have you got in your pocket? Money? What for?" he whispered.

"Mind your own business!" Dan whispered back fiercely.

"Huh! Are you saving up for a transistor?" Tom jeered, making a sly guess.

"It's nothing to do with you!" Dan muttered angrily.

"Jings! It'll take *you* years to save up for one like mine!"

"I don't want one like yours. I've got something a lot better than a transistor," Dan was goaded into replying.

"What?"

"I'm not telling you." Dan suddenly became cautious.

"I don't believe you."

"Don't bother, then!"

"If you had, you'd show me!"

"No fear! Mind your own business!" Dan retorted.

"Tom Watson and Dan Reid, stop talking!" the teacher ordered. "You will both stay in at playtime and finish that work you should be doing."

Tom Watson scowled at Dan. "I'll get you for this!" he muttered when the teacher's back was turned.

At playtime the teacher moved them to opposite sides of the room and sat at her desk while they completed their work.

"In future you do not sit next to each other," she told them. "I will not have chatter in my classroom." She rose to ring the bell at the school door to call the children into lines for re-assembly.

"Suits me, you silly kid!" Tom Watson jeered.

"Suits me, too. I don't *want* to talk to you," Dan told Tom.

All the same, Tom Watson was still inquisitive about the

money in Dan's pocket and about Dan's remark: "I've got something a lot better."

When morning school ended Tom Watson shadowed Dan along by Fidlers Green and Prior Lane into the Market Place. There he watched him stop outside Mrs Kerr's shop and count his money. Apparently satisfied, Dan stepped into the shop. Tom Watson waited outside. When Dan came out with two tins of condensed milk under his arm, Tom Watson gave a snort of frustration.

"So all that fuss about your money was just because you had to go shopping for your grandmother, you daftie! You were just making up that yarn about something better than my transistor."

"I was not!" Dan said stoutly. "And I'm *not* telling you, nosey!"

Tom Watson struck him on the arm and the tins Dan was carrying went clattering and rolling into the gutter. Attracted by the noise, Mrs Kerr suddenly appeared at the shop door. She had observed the encounter through the window.

"What are you doing, Tom Watson, you great bully?" she demanded. "Don't you come fighting and brawling outside my shop! Any more of this and I'll tell your Pa!"

Tom Watson knew Mrs Kerr meant what she said and that she bought some of her supplies through his father. He made no reply, but glowered sullenly at her.

Dan picked up one of the tins and made to go after the other which had rolled into the road but Mrs Kerr stopped him.

"No! I saw what happened. *You* pick that one up, Tom Watson, and give it to Dan."

Tom looked for a moment as if he might refuse, then he thought better of it. Mrs Kerr would certainly tell his father.

Red with temper, he went after the second tin and thrust it roughly under Dan's arm.

"Now, be off home with both of you and no more nonsense!" Mrs Kerr ordered.

The boys went their separate ways, hating each other.

As Dan neared the cottage he had another problem. *One* tin he might manage to smuggle into the house but *two* would not be easy. His pockets would bulge on either side and be sure to attract attention. Besides, he would have to smuggle one out again if he wanted to feed his seal. He had better hide one tin first: but where?

In the yard beside the cottage was an old water-butt into which a drainpipe carried the water from the roof. Dan tiptoed to the back-kitchen window. His grandmother was not there. From the clatter of the plates in the living-room he knew she must be setting the table. Quick as thought he thrust the tin up the pipe and prayed there would be no heavy rain to dislodge it in the next few hours. Now to get rid of the other tin before his grandmother returned from the living-room! The pans were bubbling on the stove and in another minute his mother would be home from the mead factory. Dan darted indoors and through to the back-kitchen. Luckily the cupboard door already stood wide open. Dan remembered the tin came from the top shelf but there was no time to move the wooden chair and stand on it. He pulled the tin from his pocket and pushed it behind the flour and sugar on the bottom shelf. It would have to stay there till he could get an opportunity to shift it again. Just as he had disposed of it, his mother came through the door and his grandmother appeared.

"Come on, both of you! Your broth's ready." She moved towards the stove.

As they took their seats at the table Dan's mother looked at him. "Oh, Dan, you untidy lad! Your pocket's half hanging out of your jeans. What have you been doing with it?"

"Looking for my handkerchief. My mouth-organ was on top of it." Dan produced a rather grubby handkerchief which his mother promptly seized.

"Give me that and go and get a clean one," she said.

"If he can find one," his grandmother remarked darkly. "A right state his drawer is in! It's like a pig's breakfast with socks, shirts and handkerchiefs all mixed up. *And* you never made your bed this morning either, Aidan," she added accusingly.

"I hope you didn't spoil him by going and making it for him," Dan's mother said.

"Well, no, I didn't, Jenny. I know it's your instructions that the children must make their own beds. But let him get his dinner now. There's no time for bed-making before he goes back to school."

"Then you come straight home at tea-time, Dan, and make it before we have our supper," his mother said firmly. "*And* you tidy up your chest of drawers too. I shall come to see it before you sit down to your supper."

Dan drew in his breath sharply. He had planned to rush down to the lime kilns straight from school before it grew too dark and give the seal its feed of condensed milk. Now there would be no time before the evening meal when his father and grandfather came home from the fishing. Dan felt desperate. *Somehow* he must get along to his seal, even if he went in the dead of night. If he failed, the baby seal might perish of hunger.

# 6     ADVENTURES IN THE NIGHT

After supper that evening Dan got up from the table while the others were still chatting. First he went quietly into the back-kitchen and collected a very large old spoon that his grandmother used to stir the broth. Then he went to lift his anorak from the peg in the passage. He was passing the open door of the living-room when his father called to him. "Where are you off to, Dan?"

"Well—er—just to see a friend," Dan stammered. After all, the seal was a kind of friend.

"It's a bit late, isn't it?" his mother said, glancing at the clock.

"Have you done your homework, son?" his father asked.

"Well—er—sort of—" Dan admitted.

"'Sort of' isn't good enough. Get your books out on the table and go over it again," Peter Reid said firmly.

Reluctantly Dan got out his books.

"I'll hear your spelling when you're ready, Dan," his grandfather offered. He could see Dan was troubled about something and he wondered what it was. No doubt in his own time Dan would tell him. There was a close bond between them, but Grandpa Reid never forced Dan's confidence. He knew Dan would come to him for help if he needed it.

At last the homework was finished. Dan yawned several times.

"You're tired, Aidan," Grandma Reid said kindly. "Why don't you away to your bed? You're yawning fit to swallow me up, as if you'd been awake all last night."

Dan felt he could fall asleep on his feet, but in another few hours he would have to be up again. He said "Goodnight" and stumbled up the stairs to his bedroom, threw off his clothes, switched off the light and fell into bed. In a couple of minutes he was fast asleep.

He was wakened by the moonlight streaming into his room, casting its beams across his face, for he had forgotten to draw the curtains. He was still in a haze of sleep. There was something he had to do. What was it? The sound of the sea dragging on the beach reminded him. The seal! It would be hungry again. He *must* go to it. In the light of the full moon he looked at his wrist watch. It was half-past three in the morning.

Dan flung on his jeans and a thick sweater, then with his wellingtons in his hand he went down the stairs. All was quiet. Outside the living-room door he paused and listened. No creaking sound came from the box-bed in the recess where his grandparents slept. Carefully he lifted his anorak from the hook in the passage and slipped his arms into it. Now to open the outer door without any noise! He grasped the big key firmly in his hand and blessed his grandfather who kept the locks oiled with his ever-ready oil can. It turned without so much as a squeak. Gently he lifted the latch and in another moment the door swung open. Silently Dan stepped out into the darkness, drew the door to him and dropped the latch into position. He could not prevent its giving a click. Once round the corner of the house he pulled on his boots, bent to collect the tin he had thrust up the pipe and pushed it into his anorak pocket. Then he started running like the wind along the shore road.

Back in the cottage Grandpa Reid woke suddenly and sat

face with staring eyes peered at him in the light of the torch, like a monk with a cowl round his head. Dan gasped with horror and almost dropped his torch. The face came nearer, breathed down his neck, then let out a loud whinneying sound!

"It's a *horse*!" Dan cried. "Just the horse that Farmer Smith grazes on the field below and somehow it's got through the fence and on to the hill."

The horse nuzzled him round the neck as if it had found a welcome friend.

"You shouldn't be up here, you know," Dan said. "You ought to be in the field down there." He took the horse gently by the mane and led it down the hill towards the field.

"Back to your pasture!" he directed, and gave the horse a slap on its flank. The horse gave another neigh of indignation, then disappeared into the night.

Dan began to retrace his footsteps carefully. He almost set his foot in a cow-pat, for cows were grazed on the hill, too, in the daytime.

"Jings!" he exclaimed in disgust. "I'd better not get *that* muck on my boots and carry it into the house, or there'd be questions asked."

At last, cautious step by cautious step, he made the steep descent to the shore. He passed the three entrances to the kiln on the eastern side, deeper pits of darkness in the dark gloom, then rounded the corner of the kilns to the little beach of pebbles and mossy grass at Castle Point.

"I'd better let the seal know I'm coming," he said to himself, and pulled his mouth-organ out of his pocket. The strains of *Onward Christian Soldiers!* rang out over the sea. For a minute or two there was no reply, then there came an answering bleating note from inside the centre lime kiln.

Dan no longer had any fear of entering the dark cave-like opening. The seal was still alive. With his torch in one hand he advanced, still playing the mouth-organ. The seal weakly tried to raise a flipper as if in greeting. Dan set his torch down upon a stone with his mouth-organ and tugged the tin of condensed milk out of his pocket along with the tin-opener. In a jiffy he had the tin open. He held it up to the seal's mouth. It sniffed at it, gave a pitiful little wail, but did not try to put its tongue inside the tin.

"Oh, aren't you a real baby!" Dan said. "You want it put right into your mouth, don't you?"

He dipped his fingers in the milk and rubbed them over the seal's whiskers and smeared the milk over its mouth. The seal hardly seemed to have the strength to lick it off. It was plain to Dan that the little creature was much weaker.

"If I can't get food into you, you'll die!" Dan declared desperately. He thrust the spoon into the milk, then daubed the seal's mouth with it. Again the seal licked around its whiskers. Next time Dan held the full spoon of milk to the seal's mouth. To Dan's surprise the seal opened its mouth and licked the milk off the spoon!

"Gosh! You're learning! You'll be a spoon-fed baby yet!" Dan cried with delight.

He advanced the spoonful of milk again and again. The seal seemed to have got the idea and sucked at the spoon each time. Sometimes, of course, some of the milk was spilled when the seal put its mouth to the spoon, but it took half a dozen spoonsful before it seemed to tire.

"I wish there was a quicker way of getting it into you," Dan said. He waited patiently for a few minutes, then tried the spoon again. Once more the little seal sucked off the milk, this time so eagerly that the long spoon almost disappeared down its throat.

"Steady on!" Dan cried, pulling the spoon back just in time. "That's not for eating!"

It took a very long time, but at last the tin of milk was

empty. Some of it had been spilled in the feeding, but quite a lot of it had gone down the seal's throat. The hungry little creature tried to raise its flippers and move forward as if to ask for more.

"Still hungry, are you?" Dan asked. "Oh, there's still some left in the tin I put under the stone. Let's see if you can take that too."

The seal managed to take the small amount that remained in the old tin and still opened its mouth for more!

"I'm sorry, but that's all," Dan said, stroking its furry back. "You've had almost one and a half tins. What on earth am I to do about it? I'll soon have spent all the money in my money box on tins of milk and what'll I do then?"

He patted and stroked the little seal, and it nestled close to him, nuzzling him gently, as if trusting him. Dan felt a big wave of love for the helpless little creature.

"You've only got me, haven't you?" Dan spoke gently. "Never mind! Somehow we'll find a way to keep you fed."

He glanced out of the kiln at the deep heaving darkness of the sea. The moon came from behind a cloud and made an edge of phosphorescent whiteness to the waves. In the east, low on the horizon, the sky seemed lighter.

"It's time I was back in my bed before Dad gets up," Dan reminded himself. He gave a final friendly pat to the little seal. "I'll be coming back," he promised and rose to his feet. The seal made a feeble attempt to follow him and raised itself slightly on its flippers, then sank back, still too weak to move further.

Dan buried the condensed milk tins under some stones, then made his way up the grass track, round the base of the castle mound and along by the little road bordering the summer car park. He reached the beach by the shore of the Ouse and at last he came to his own cottage.

"Now to get in as quietly as I came out," he said to himself and pressed down the latch of the door handle, but the door would not open. Once more he tried, but the door remained closed. Dan looked at it in dismay.

"It must be locked! Now what'll I do?" he whispered.

A chill dawn wind came from the sea and he shivered. He faced round to the water, at a loss. "There's only the shed," he reminded himself. "I'll be out of the wind there and I can watch the house, and when they open the door in the morning maybe I can slip in without anyone seeing me."

He crossed the grass to the stony beach and felt in the hollow for the key. Another minute and he was out of the wind. He closed the door of the shed quietly, then took out his torch and shone it about him. In the corner was a pile of folded nets. Suddenly Dan felt very tired as he sank into them. They made a soft bed and Dan curled up among them, drawing a piece of old sail-cloth over him. In no time at all, he was fast asleep.

When he awoke, the grey light of a November morning was in the small window and the sun was filtering through the clouds on the eastern horizon. Dan opened the shed door very slowly and cautiously and looked across the grassy beach to the cottage. Already there was a light in the living-room window.

"Now to get in without being seen. I do hope they've not started breakfast," Dan murmured to himself. He closed the shed door without a sound and crept like a burglar over the grass.

Just at the moment that Dan emerged from the shed Grandpa Reid happened to look out of the living-room window towards the harbour. He saw the small shadowy figure come out of the shed and close the door.

"Who's that?" he said sharply, but Grandma Reid did not hear him as she was clattering the pans in the back-

kitchen, preparing the breakfast. Grandpa Reid rubbed his eyes as the small figure approached the door. "Why, it's Dan!" he said to himself. "What's the lad doing in the shed so early in the morning? I never heard him go out when I went to unlock the door."

He heard the door open quietly and the stealthy footsteps go up the stairs.

"What's he been up to?" Grandpa asked himself. "I'll wait till I call him for breakfast and then perhaps he'll tell me."

Twenty minutes later he mounted the stairs to arouse the household. Dan's father and mother were already astir, but when Grandpa reached the attic bedroom Dan was sprawled on his bed, fully clothed but fast asleep! Grandpa gave an affectionate shake of his head towards the boy. "He'll have some reason for being out so early. He'll tell me in his own time, no doubt. I'll not say anything about it to the others."

There was a great bond of friendship and trust between Dan and his grandfather, and Grandpa Reid had no wish to get Dan into trouble. Gently he stroked the boy's head.

"Come on, Dan! Time to get up!"

Dan opened his eyes sleepily.

"You've got your clothes on," Grandpa said. "You must have fallen asleep again after dressing."

"I must have done," Dan muttered guiltily. After all, it was true. He *had* fallen asleep after dressing, but it was a long time earlier in the night that he had dressed.

Grandpa Reid gave him a sharp look. Dan was surely hiding something. Ah, well, it would come out some time, Grandpa thought. "Well, come on, laddie!" he urged Dan aloud. "Your Grandma will be pouring the porridge for you in a minute or two."

The older ones were all seated at the table when Dan clattered down the stairs after hastily washing his face and pulling a comb through his tousled hair. His porridge was set at his place and already cooling. Dan's mother gave him a quick look.

"Dan, did you fold your clothes properly last night? They're all crumpled as if you'd slept in them."

"Sorry!" Dan said. "Maybe I forgot to fold them."

Grandpa Reid looked sharply across at him. Surely Dan had not slept in his clothes last night? Why? He kept his thoughts to himself, however.

Dan's mother had not finished, though. She was looking

at his boots. "Your boots are dirty. Surely you cleaned them last night? Didn't I see you go into the back-kitchen to clean them?"

It was a rule in the Reid household that boots and shoes must be cleaned the night before, ready for the morning.

"Er—yes. Maybe I didn't do them very well," Dan stammered.

"Then you go and do them now before you eat your porridge," his father ordered. "I will not have you being slovenly, Dan. Any more of this nonsense and there's no pocket money for you this week!"

Dan took a deep breath. No pocket money! That would mean there would be no condensed milk for his seal.

"I—I'll be more careful," he promised as he retreated to the back-kitchen.

Before he went to school he rushed up the stairs and prised out the last of his money from his money box. Enough for two more tins of condensed milk, that was all! What would he do next? In his own mind he put up a desperate prayer for help to keep his seal alive. Then, slamming the door behind him, he was away like the wind to school, anxious that he should not add being late to his other misdoings.

"That bairn! Off he goes at the last moment. He's getting a right sleepy head in the mornings," Grandma Reid remarked.

"Sometimes I think he doesn't get sleep enough," Grandpa Reid said darkly. He was remembering that he had found the outer door unlocked last night. Had Dan unlocked it and gone out? Had he slept in the boat shed? Grandpa, however, kept his thoughts to himself. Time would tell, or Dan would, he felt sure.

# 7     SURPRISES FOR TOM WATSON AND DAN

Dan decided he would not risk any more excursions to the lime kilns in the night. Sooner or later he would be found out, for Grandpa Reid was a light sleeper. It would be better to go in the dinner hour from school, but he would first have to buy his tins of condensed milk. It would be wiser, too, to keep the tins hidden in the lime kiln. In any case, he only had enough money left for one tin a day. He wondered anxiously if one tin would be enough for his seal and if it would ever be strong enough to go into the sea and fish for its food.

At dinner-time on Tuesday he dashed home. Grandma Reid was already putting his bowl of soup on the table. It was good thick Scotch Broth, piping hot. Dan hastily swallowed a spoonful and almost choked.

"Now, now, Aidan, don't go at your broth like a seal at a salmon. You'll scald your mouth."

Dan had already done so, but he bravely hid the fact and poured himself a glass of water, coldly welcome as it ran over his tongue. At last, sip by sip, he finished his broth. Herring and potatoes followed. The potatoes were hot too. When no one was looking, Dan smuggled a couple of them into his pocket. Why, oh why, did herrings have so many bones? Dan tried to swallow a big mouthful and gave a choking cough as the bones slid down his throat.

"Dan!" his mother exclaimed. "Stop bolting your food like that!"

Dan was forced to slow down his eating. He cast an anxious glance at the clock.

"Please may I go now?" at last he asked desperately, "I—I've something to do before school."

"Are you in trouble with the teacher?" his mother asked sharply.

"No, oh no!" Dan hoped she wouldn't ask any more questions.

His grandfather came to his rescue. "Come, Jenny, don't ask too many questions. Dan just wants a game with the other lads in the school-yard before school. You did, when you were a lassie."

"Oh, all right then," Dan's mother agreed.

Dan did not wait. He snatched up his anorak and was away with the wind at his back.

"Oh, those boys and their football!" his mother exclaimed.

Grandpa Reid was not so sure it was football, but again he said nothing.

Dan sped past the Crown and Anchor Inn and across the Market Place to Mrs Kerr's shop. The shop bell tinkled as he burst in. Mrs Kerr appeared slowly from the back premises.

"Goodness me! What a time you boys choose to come! Just when I'm at my dinner! Well, what kind of sweets do you want?"

"It isn't sweets, Mrs Kerr. I want two tins of condensed milk, please."

Mrs Kerr took it for granted that the tins were for Dan's grandmother. "What a powerful lot of candy your grandmother must be making! It'll be for the Church sale as usual?" she asked curiously.

"Huh, huh," Dan mumbled. After all, Grandma *would* be making her "Scotch Tablet" for the Church sale.

He put down the money for the tins, then thrust them into his pockets and ran as fast as he could along Fenkle Street and St Cuthbert's Square towards the Castle Hill. He was not unobserved, however. From his home near the Popple Well, Tom Watson saw him.

"Now, where's Dan Reid going?" he asked curiously.

When Dan reached the lime kiln he played a quick skirl of *Onward Christian Soldiers* on his mouth-organ and was answered by a plaintive bleat, almost like a lamb's. He dashed into the cave. The seal looked at him with eyes full of tears. Dan did not know that seals' eyes water easily and he thought the little seal was weeping.

"Oh, you poor little soul!" he cried, patting the seal. Then he opened the tin as fast as he could, smeared the seal's whiskers with the milk, watched as it licked the milk off; then he proffered the spoon. The seal seemed to know what to do this time and opened its mouth. Dan thrust in the long-handled spoon but held on like grim death lest the seal should swallow it down. One old long spoon his grandmother might not miss but she would certainly miss two, if he had to borrow another.

It took a long time to spoon the milk down the seal's throat and even then the seal was still hungry.

"One tin a day is never going to be enough," Dan told himself. "Whatever shall I do?" He could see that the baby seal was thinner and weaker.

"Oh, I don't want you to die!" Dan cried as the seal snuggled close to him, hungry for more to eat. It had learned by now that Dan was the provider of its food and looked at Dan as if he were a kind of mother. The tears rolled out of the seal's eyes, and Dan's eyes watered too.

"Oh, how shall I find food for you?" Dan exclaimed.

The tolling of the school bell at the far side of the town warned him that he had no time to waste. He hid the empty tin and the full one in a hole in the kiln floor and pulled a couple of stones forward to hide them, then ran as hard as he could up the hill. Breathless he reached Front Street: then, his heart pounding, he reached Marygate. Round the corner from Crossgates Lane, Tom Watson almost bumped into him.

"Hi, Dan Reid! You don't usually come this way to school. Where've you been?"

Dan did not answer. He sped on past the cottages and the tea-rooms, hoping to outdistance Tom Watson, but Tom still kept up with him.

Tom repeated his question. "Where've you been, Reid? To the farm?"

Dan shook his head.

"Where then?"

Stung by Tom Watson's inquisitive questioning, Dan barked out, "It's no business of yours, Tom Watson!"

Tom Watson squared up his fists, but just as he and Dan turned into Lewins Lane, the school bell gave a couple of final tinny clangs and stopped. The school lay right ahead. Both boys sprinted hard and arrived just as the teacher reached the doorstep with her hand-bell to marshal the children into a line.

Tom Watson gasped in Dan's ear, "You wait, Dan Reid! I'll find out for myself where you go!"

Dan gave a little shiver, but he stared straight ahead as they marched into school.

All that afternoon as he did his school work, Dan was in a kind of dream. At the back of his mind he wrestled all the time with the problem of his seal. It was plainly getting weaker and one tin of condensed milk a day was barely keeping it alive. Only one tin was left and Dan's money box was almost empty, and there would be no pocket money till Friday night. On Wednesday the last tin would be used. On Thursday he would have nothing to give his seal, unless he could get the replacement tin out of the cupboard again. Would Kate help him? She was coming home early on Friday—but would she arrive before the shop shut? If not there would be nothing for the seal till Saturday. Perhaps Mrs Kerr would let him have a tin on Thursday if he promised to pay her on Saturday when he would have his pocket money? But on Friday and Saturday he would need two more tins to feed the seal over the week-end. Dan felt desperate. He would *have* to tell Kate about the seal and he must be sure of getting a tin for Thursday. If only Kate could bring a tin with her! Then Dan had a bright idea. The telephone! Kate's school hostel had a telephone. If he waited till 6.0 p.m. there were cheap calls and he might get Kate then. He decided to 'phone Kate.

That evening Dan sat down immediately after his tea and did his homework. Luckily he had not got much to do that night, one sum and some spelling. He got his grandfather to check both and managed to get by without any errors.

"Good lad!" Grandpa said approvingly. "It's always better to get down to your homework right away."

Dan put his books together in his satchel, then, while the elders were discussing the prices obtained for the day's fishing, he slipped quietly out of the house.

He hurried to the Post Office in Prior Lane where there was a call box. He looked quickly about him. The street was deserted. Most of the residents were at their evening meal. In the 'phone book he found the number for Kate's school hostel, read the directions and found he must first dial 0289, the Berwick-on-Tweed code. Good! That was the same code as for the island, which meant it would come within the 35-mile limit, so he could talk to Kate for three minutes at the

cheap rate. But Kate would have to be found and brought
to the telephone so the call might cost sixpence or even more.
Dan anxiously laid all the coins he had on the shelf in the
telephone kiosk. Just three twopenny pieces left! He put up
a prayer that Kate would come promptly to the 'phone. With
a trembling finger he dialled the code number, then the
number for the hostel. The 'phone bell started ringing at the
hostel. What must he do next? Luckily, just in time, Dan
remembered he must put his money in the slot as soon as
he heard the voice answer. There! Someone was speaking.
Better put in enough money for six minutes. Dan pushed the
three twopenny pieces in the slot. The voice spoke the hostel
number again.

"Please, I want to speak to Kate Reid," Dan said.

"Who is that speaking?"

"I'm her brother, Dan Reid."

"She's having her evening meal. Can I take a message to
her?"

"Oh, *please* can she come to the 'phone? I want to speak
to her myself. It's important. Please will you tell her to hurry!
I haven't any money left for another call."

Dan sounded so desperate that the "house-mother" went
to fetch Kate. The seconds ticked away as Dan clutched the
'phone to his ear. Three minutes gone already! Would Kate
never come? At last Dan heard running footsteps and the
'phone was lifted.

"Kate!" Dan gasped.

"Hullo! What's up? Anything wrong at home?" Kate
sounded breathless and anxious.

"No, nothing's wrong."

"Why are you 'phoning then?"

"*Listen*, Kate, please! When you come home will you bring
a tin of condensed milk with you? Two, if you have the
money."

"Condensed milk?" Kate sounded very surprised. "Who wants it? Grandma? Hasn't Mrs Kerr got any at the shop?"

"No, not Grandma! *I* want it, Kate. Please don't tell anyone at home. Just give me the tins quietly."

"What do you want them for?"

"I can't tell you now. I'll tell you when you get home."

"Tell me *now*!" Kate demanded.

"Oh, Kate, I can't. There isn't time. Please, please bring the tins with you," Dan pleaded. "I *need* them."

"Oh, all right! But I shan't hand them over till you've told me."

There was a clicking sound; time ran out and the 'phone went dead. Dan set it back again on its cradle. At least he had got through to Kate and he felt sure Kate would keep her word. But now there was no money left in his pocket or in his money box. After tomorrow it all depended whether Mrs Kerr would let him have "tick", or credit, till Saturday.

On Wednesday Dan swallowed his midday dinner as quickly as possible, excused himself and ran out of the house as fast as he could.

"That laddie! He'll die of indigestion," Grandma said disapprovingly. "I didna' ken he was that keen on football."

"Maybe it's not the football," Grandpa Reid said thoughtfully. "Maybe he's interested in some birds."

"Och! You and Aidan! What a pair you are for birds and fishes!" Grandma Reid declared.

Dan approached the lime kilns by the shore path, for the tide was low enough to let him get across the rocks. As he climbed up the little beach towards the entrance to the kiln he sounded the first notes of his signature tune to tell the seal of his coming. Then he stopped abruptly, just as the seal gave its answering wail. Other music was coming from the path round the side of the kiln, *pop* music! Dan's heart filled with dread as round the corner came Tom Watson with his radio transistor playing at full blast.

"Hullo! You didn't think I'd find you here, did you?" Tom Watson jeered at him. He glanced at the mouth-organ in Dan's hand. "What's that thing?"

"My mouth-organ," Dan said boldly, retreating from the entrance to the lime kiln and away from Tom Watson. On no account must he betray to Tom Watson that his seal was inside the kiln. "I come down here to practise it quietly," he explained. All the time he moved away from the kiln towards the path over the rocks and Tom Watson followed him.

"You're just a silly kid!" Tom Watson sneered at him. "Hand that thing over to me."

"No!" Dan said fiercely. "I'll fight you first." He kept moving away from the lime kiln until he was almost under the corner where the fulmar petrels had their nest. The two parent petrels squawked loudly.

Tom Watson picked up a stone and flung it at Dan but it missed him and hit the kiln corner just below the petrels' nest. The birds fluttered indignantly. Dan gave a glance at them. So did Tom Watson. His eyes narrowed craftily. He knew about Dan's passion for birds.

"Oh, so that's your game, is it?" he snarled. "Got some pet sea-birds up there, have you? It's those birds you come to see, not to play that daft mouth-organ. I'll soon stop that!" Tom Watson flung another stone, this time at the nest. The fulmar petrels flew out, fluttering round the nest and squawking angrily.

"Leave them alone!" Dan shouted. "They're rare birds. They're fulmar petrels."

"Oh, rare birds are they?" Tom Watson mocked him. "I bet their eggs would fetch a good price in Berwick."

"They haven't got eggs in November. The chicks hatched

in the summer," Dan told him. He did not want Tom Watson to injure the birds or their nest.

"I don't believe you!" Tom Watson said. "I'm going up to see and if they've got chicks I'll wring their stupid necks."

There was a steep sloping path which led upwards almost to the gable of the lime kiln where the birds were nesting. With his transistor still slung about his neck, Tom Watson began to climb. There were foot-holds in the crumbling stonework and he began the last easy ascent to the nest. The fulmar petrels grew angrier and fluttered about his head as though warning him to turn back. They withdrew to their nest and awaited him with outstretched necks and pointing beaks. They did not even utter a cry, but just waited ominously.

"Come down before they peck your eyes out," Dan cried to him.

"Get away! I'll chuck their nest down first," Tom Watson shouted, and drew himself up level with the nest and stretched out a hand towards it. Then, with one accord, the two parent petrels went in to the attack. There was a snorting, sneezing sound and from the tube-like nostrils on each beak a filthy stream of partly digested food was squirted over Tom Watson! Some of it hit him in the face but, luckily for him, missed his eyes. Most of it streamed over his pull-over and anorak. It was foul-smelling and horrid slime, for fulmar petrels feed on fatty fish like herrings and mackerel which they digest into a kind of oil. To vomit this over their enemies is their way of defence.

Tom Watson, looking quite green and sick, came down from the nest, slithering the last part of the way down the slippery path. Dan looked at him and laughed aloud.

"That'll teach you to leave those birds alone, Tom Watson. You've only got what you asked for. Jings! If you could only see the mess you're in! It looks like you've been sick all over yourself."

"I'll murder you!" Tom Watson yelled and took a step towards Dan, but suddenly he *did* feel sick.

"You'd better go home and get washed and changed," Dan advised him from a safe distance. "The teacher'll not have you in school smelling like that. You—you *stink*!"

Dan half expected Tom Watson to go for him and clenched his fists ready but, to his surprise, Tom Watson suddenly turned and ran along the pathway over the rocks towards the Ouse and his home. Dan would have been amazed had he known his enemy was near to tears.

As soon as Tom Watson had disappeared Dan wasted no time in beginning to feed his seal. Luckily the seal seemed to know what was required of it and sucked away at the spoonful of milk. For all that, Dan could see that the poor creature was weaker. One tin of condensed milk a day was not going to keep it alive. He went back to school feeling decidedly low in spirits.

Tom Watson came to school late, looking very sheepish. He made some muttered excuse to the teacher.

"Fell in a puddle, did you, and had to change your clothes?" the teacher said. "You should look where you're going, Tom Watson." She waved him impatiently to his place.

Dan could hardly resist a guffaw as Tom Watson took his seat.

As he passed Dan, Tom Watson whispered fiercely, "I'll get you for this, Dan Reid. *And* those birds!"

"Away, you still stink!" Dan pretended to hold his nose.

Luckily the teacher had her back to him as she was writing on the blackboard.

Wednesday was early-closing day and Mrs Kerr's shop would be shut, so Dan could not call there on his way home to get his tin of condensed milk. In any case, he had no money left in his pocket. It would be Friday afternoon before Kate arrived with the two tins of milk, if she managed to get them. That meant he must wait until Saturday before he could feed the seal again. Would it survive two days without any food? Dan was very doubtful. He *must* call at Mrs Kerr's shop early in the morning and coax her into letting him have another tin of milk on his promise to pay her on Saturday.

Dan was on the doorstep of Mrs Kerr's shop when she unbolted the door in the morning.

"Mrs Kerr, please will you let me have a tin of condensed milk? I ... I've come without my money, but if you'll let me have it, I promise I'll bring the money on Saturday morning, really I will!"

Mrs Kerr looked at him curiously and hesitated.

"Please, Mrs Kerr!" Dan urged her. "Please let me have it now or I'll be late for school."

Mrs Kerr knew Dan for an honest boy, but he had never asked for "tick" before. The Reids were good customers and paid for everything over the counter. There would be no harm, however, in letting Dan have one tin, she thought. She reached for the tin from the shelf behind her.

"There you are, Dan! That's my last tin, though, till I get a fresh supply. You've surely cleaned out my stock this week."

Dan felt this announcement like a blow to his heart, but he snatched up the tin and stammered, "Thank you. I'll be back with the money on Saturday," and was gone like the wind.

That morning Grandpa Reid took a stroll along to the shop for some tobacco.

"Hullo, Mr Reid!" Mrs Kerr greeted him. "Don't tell me *you've* come for a tin of condensed milk!"

"No, why should I?" Grandpa Reid looked mystified.

"A powerful lot of fudge Mrs Reid must be making for the Church sale!"

"Fudge?" Grandpa lifted his eyebrows.

"Aye, her special candy, 'Scotch Tablet' she calls it. Dan's been in every day this week, and last week-end too, for tins of condensed milk. I've not a tin left. I gave Dan my last one this morning. I'll have to get some more in stock."

Grandpa thought hard. Grandma Reid had certainly not been making "tablet" or he would have smelt it cooking. Besides, she always poured it into tins and left it in the back-kitchen to cool, and then cut it up, giving him a piece to taste, and Dan one too. There was a mystery about this.

"Mm!" Grandpa commented. "I'll find out." But he said no more.

When he got back to the cottage he asked Grandma Reid, "Have you made your 'tablet' for the Church sale yet?"

"Michty me, no! It's far too soon. I only make it a couple of days beforehand."

"Have you got your condensed milk in, then?"

"Only one tin in the cupboard," Grandma told him. "I'd better get another tin in, though. What made you ask?"

"Oh, I just wondered," Grandpa Reid said, putting on a vague air. "Mrs Kerr was asking and talking of getting some tins in stock. She's sold out of it."

Grandma Reid asked no questions and bustled away to her baking, but Grandpa Reid puffed at his pipe and thought hard.

"There was the door unlocked one night and Dan found asleep in his clothes. And he throws his dinner down his throat every day and rushes away somewhere. And now all these tins of condensed milk? What is it that little lad is up to? It might be a wise idea to find out," he said to himself.

# 8

At dinner time Dan gobbled his food again quicker than ever. Grandpa watched him on the quiet. In the middle of the meal Grandma said, "I'd meant to make a bean and bacon pie for tea but I can't find the tin-opener anywhere to open the can of beans. Have you got it on the boat?" she asked Grandpa.

Grandpa shook his head. "No, we've had no occasion to open a tin."

"And that old long-handled spoon I use for the broth has gone missing too," Grandma remarked, vexed.

"Most likely you've popped it in a drawer somewhere," Dan's mother said. "It'll turn up when you're not looking for it."

Dan said nothing, but he could not suppress the guilty flush that overspread his face. He bent his head lower over his plate. Grandpa noticed but he made no remark. He thought to himself, "Tins of condensed milk, a tin-opener and the long spoon. What does it all add up to? Surely Dan's not devouring a tin of condensed milk every day? He'd make himself sick. He seems to have a hearty boy's appetite just as usual, though." Aloud he asked Dan, "How's the mouth-organ doing, Dan?"

"Oh, fine, Grandpa, fine," Dan said hastily. "I can play several tunes now."

"Still practising over by the lime kilns?"

Dan gave his grandfather a swift glance, but Grandpa Reid was quietly eating his dinner, not even looking Dan's way.

"Yes," Dan said. So Grandpa had watched him going round the Ouse to Castle Point and thought he was just going to play his mouth-organ.

"I'll come along and hear you some time," Grandpa said casually.

Dan was startled by this announcement. For a moment he did not know what to say, then he stammered, "I—I'm not awfully good yet. Perhaps you should wait a bit—"

"Mm—mm!" Grandpa nodded. But he took note of Dan's hesitation.

Dan hurried away from the table as soon as he could be excused. He felt a little worried. Questions about the tin-opener and the spoon! Sooner or later Grandma would ask him a direct question about them and Dan was not a boy who told lies. He was desperately anxious to get to the seal too. Was it still alive? He remembered Tom Watson's threat to "get" him and wondered if he was already down at the Castle Point, could even have found the seal? He broke into a run, scrambling over the rocks and the grassy pathway to the kilns. No one was around. He breathed a sigh of relief, brought out his mouth-organ and gave a flourish on it. To his joy a weak but plaintive sound answered him from the kiln. The seal was still alive.

Dan was just about to plunge into the shadowy depths of the kiln when a figure came round the corner by the upper path. It was Tom Watson! In his hands he carried a loop of leather and elastic. Dan recognised it for Tom Watson's secret weapon, a *sling*.

"Hi, you!" shouted Tom Watson, and a pebble hit Dan on the shoulder. Dan might have taken to his heels, but he knew he would have to face up to Tom Watson if he was to keep him from discovering the seal.

"You rotten thing, Tom Watson!" he shouted angrily.

Tom Watson picked up another pebble, a larger one this time. Dan dodged quickly into one of the entrances to the kiln, but *not* the one where his seal was lying.

"Hide, would you?" Tom Watson jeered at him. "This stone isn't for *you*. I'll deal with you later when I've killed those filthy birds up there."

He aimed his sling at the fulmar petrels' nest. The pebble hit a corner of the nest but the birds rose from it unhurt, making angry cries and flapping their wings. Tom Watson stooped to pick up another pebble, but before he could fit it into his sling, Dan was upon him.

"Leave those birds alone!" Dan shouted angrily, but Watson again took aim. Before he could let fly the pebble, however, Dan had torn the sling out of his hand and with a powerful heave, flung it as far out into the bay as he could.

"If you want your sling back you can swim for it, Tom Watson!" he cried.

Tom Watson swung round and struck at Dan with his fist, but Dan quickly side-stepped so that the blow missed his face and hit his shoulder. He countered with a smack in the ribs which stopped Tom Watson in his tracks. The two boys circled round each other like boxers with fists at the ready, then Tom, infuriated, dashed at Dan with arms flailing. He was bigger and heavier than Dan, and Dan might have got the worst of the attack if Tom Watson had not tripped over a jutting piece of rock. Down he went with Dan on top of him. The two boys scuffled, rolling round on the beach, pounding each other with their fists. Then, out of Dan's pocket fell his mouth-organ! Dan did not see it but Tom Watson did. He let go of Dan for a moment, snatched it up, leaped to his feet and held it aloft.

"This goes after my sling!" he shouted and lifted his arm to throw the mouth-organ into the waves.

Dan flew at him and seized his arm, forgetting all fear in his anxiety to wrest the precious mouth-organ from Watson's grip. Tom Watson still held it aloft but now he only had one arm at liberty to withstand Dan's attack. Dan danced round him, pummelling at his ribs, trying to reach the mouth-organ, but Tom's longer arm defeated him. Dan's blows, however, prevented him from giving the full swing to his arm to send the mouth-organ hurtling into the waves. He made an attempt to throw it, but Dan's grab at his arm made his aim fall short and the mouth-organ fell on the shingle a few yards away. Both boys darted to pick it up again, falling over each other and fighting on the ground as they tried to reach it. There was no knowing how the fight might have ended, but suddenly there was a shout and a wrathful figure descended on them, pulled them apart, then heaved each boy to his feet by a powerful grip on the necks of their jerkins. It was Grandfather Reid!

"What's going on here?" he demanded. "What's the fight about?" Then he spied the bright glint of the mouth-organ among the pebbles.

"Is that your mouth-organ, Dan?" He still kept hold of both boys. Dan nodded.

"Was Tom Watson trying to throw it into the sea? I saw it in his hand as I came by the cliff."

Again Dan nodded.

"Why did you do that?" Grandpa demanded. "What had Dan done to you?"

"He threw my sling into the sea," Tom Watson said sullenly.

"Did you, Dan?"

"Yes, Grandpa," Dan admitted.

"Why did you do that?"

Dan did not reply for he did not wish to tell tales, but just then the fulmar petrels answered for him. Once more they rose squawking from their nest, flapping their wings. Both boys could not help giving a quick glance at them. In an instant Grandpa Reid grasped why Dan had thrown the sling into the sea.

"Were you throwing pebbles at those birds?" he asked Tom Watson sternly.

"What does it matter if I was?" Tom asked defiantly.

"Just this, Tom Watson. Those birds are rare birds, fulmar petrels. You kill one of them and you'll find yourself in trouble with the police. What's more, my lad, you'll find yourself in trouble with *me*. Let me catch you at it and I'll frog-march you home and let your father know what you've been up to." He knew Tom Watson stood in awe of his father who would take a dim view of anything that upset the good feeling of the islanders towards him and his trade.

Tom Watson looked at Dan and his grandfather sullenly. "He shouldn't have thrown away my sling," he muttered.

"Now, take heed, my lad," Grandpa warned him. "If I catch you interfering with those birds again there'll be worse coming to you than losing your sling. Now, be off home with you!"

Grandpa Reid released his hold on Tom, who needed no further warning. He scurried away, scrambling over the rocks as fast as he could go. Grandpa Reid watched him disappear round the corner of the lime kilns.

"Pick up your mouth-organ, Dan," he said.

Dan hurried to retrieve it, dusted the sand off it and looked it over carefully for any signs of damage.

"Is it all right?" Grandpa asked.

"Yes." Dan gave a sigh of relief.

"Then let me hear you play a tune on it."

Dan hesitated a moment, then put the instrument to his

mouth and played the opening bars of *The Bluebells of Scotland.* Suddenly, from within the lime kiln, came a feeble pitiful bleating-moaning sound.

"What's that?" Grandpa exclaimed.

Dan broke off his tune. "It—it's my seal," he stammered.

"*Your seal?*"

"It—it's just a baby seal that's got stranded."

Grandpa strode into the dark recess of the lime kiln, Dan at his heels. Dan brought out his pocket torch. In its light the little seal looked up at them, tears brimming its limpid eyes.

"Mercy me!" Grandpa exclaimed. "How long has this been here?"

"About a week," Dan gulped. "It—it's awful hungry."

Grandpa put two and two together and quickly made four: all those tins of condensed milk; the tin-opener and the missing spoon; Dan's going out in the night.

"Have you been feeding it? he asked.

"Trying to," Dan said sadly.

"On tinned milk?"

Dan nodded unhappily. "Yes, but it doesn't seem enough and now Mrs Kerr hasn't any more in her shop and I owe her for the last tin and when Kate comes home tomorrow I'll owe her for two more, and by then it might be too late and the seal might have died of starvation." Dan poured it all out in a flood of misery.

Grandpa said no word of rebuke. Instead he rumpled Dan's hair in rough affection. "Let's have a look at the little chap—or lady," he said.

He stroked the seal's sides and felt at them gently. "It's lost a lot of its fat and its skin is dry and shrivelled," he said.

"Oh, Grandpa, will it die after all?"

"It will unless we can get some more food into it,"

Grandpa replied grimly. "What have you been giving it? Just condensed milk?"

"Yes."

"That's not enough by itself. The seal-mother's milk is far richer and has oil and fat in it. Perhaps we might try a mixture of condensed milk and cod-liver oil," Grandpa thought aloud.

"We?" Dan exclaimed. "Do you mean you'll help, Grandpa?"

"Why, of course, Dan!"

Dan's tears really did come then. "Oh, oh, and I was so afraid you might be angry and kill it."

Grandpa looked at him in astonishment. "What? Kill a poor helpless little thing like that? Surely you know me better than that, Dan? That was daft!"

"I know! I know! I wish now I'd told you about it at the very beginning," Dan almost sobbed.

"Aye, well, let's hope you haven't left it too late now. I'll see what I can do." Grandpa looked at his watch. "Jings!

Listen! That's the school bell. Away with you if you don't want to be late and be kept in. Leave feeding the seal to me."

Dan was already jumping across the rocks to the shore path when Grandpa called after him, "And take no nonsense from that Tom Watson. Just give him a skelp if he starts anything." Then he chuckled to himself, "But from what I saw I think you're well able to stand up for yourself, Dannie lad! And now to tackle this problem!" He stroked the little seal again. "Let's hope you're tougher than you look."

When Dan got home from afternoon school he found Grandpa looking out for him. "Come with me, Dan," he said. He led Dan to the shed on the shore. There he took out a lantern that they used on the boat. "This will give a better light than a pocket torch," he told Dan. He also picked up a bass bag in which they carried fish for bait.

"What have you got in there?" Dan asked.

"You'll soon see," Grandpa said with a grin. "Come on, now! Let's hurry. If we're not back for tea your Grandma will have something to say."

They set off along the shore for the lime kilns.

"Play your mouth-organ to let the little creature know we're coming," Grandpa suggested. "It seems to like your signature tune."

After a few bars of *Onward Christian Soldiers*, there came the answering wail, but it was very feeble. When they entered the lime kiln the seal looked at them with dull eyes. It was very weak indeed.

"Now to try and get this stuff into it," Grandpa said. From the bass bag he produced a thermos flask containing a coffee-coloured mixture.

"What's that?" Dan asked in surprise.

"It's a mixture of condensed milk and cod-liver oil warmed just slightly," Grandpa told him.

"But Mrs Kerr had no condensed milk left!" Dan exclaimed, puzzled.

"True! But I had a couple of tins aboard the 'Jenny'. I got a jar of cod-liver oil and mixed it in. This makes a richer mixture, warm and more like the seal-mother's milk. I warmed it over the stove in the 'Jenny's' galley, so—well so as to be out of your Grandma's way," Grandpa said rather guiltily.

Dan was peering into the bag. "But what's this other thing? Isn't it what Grandma uses to baste the meat when she's roasting it?"

"Right first time, Dan."

The baster was a hard white plastic tube about thirty centimetres long. At its bottom end it was only about a centimetre wide but it broadened to a long barrel, several centimetres in diameter. This barrel was marked in fluid ounces, from one-quarter to one ounce. At the wide end was a strong rubber bulb which fitted very closely over the plastic tube.

"But what's the baster for?" Dan asked.

"To try an experiment in feeding the seal. Mind you, it may not work."

"But what if Grandma misses the baster?" Dan asked.

"She won't. Not till Sunday! I can have it back in time

for her to baste the Sunday joint." Grandpa gave Dan the smile of a fellow conspirator. "Now, Dan, the seal knows you and expects the food from you, so go ahead as you have been doing, letting it lick this mixture off the spoon. We've got to persuade him—or maybe her—to accept this food which is just a bit different."

Dan dipped his finger in the mixture and licked one finger first. "Ugh! It tastes queer. It would make me sick!"

"Maybe, but let's hope the seal will like it."

Dan laced the seal's whiskers with the mixture and after a slight hesitation, the seal licked it off. After that Dan tried some of the mixture on the spoon. The seal accepted the spoon too, but Dan had to hold on tight to the handle to prevent the seal swallowing it as well.

"Well, the seal's taken to the new mixture," Grandpa said, "but it would take us a terrible long time to spoon all this lot down its throat and quite a bit of it gets dribbled down its chest and wasted. We'll try my experiment now."

Grandpa took up the baster and expelled the air by squeezing the tube, then dipped it into the mixture and drew the rich milk up into the tube by letting the bulb expand again in his hand. He handed the full baster to Dan.

"Now see if you can persuade the seal to take the end of the baster in its mouth."

Dan tried to get the seal to open its mouth, but it kept it firmly closed and drew its head back.

"Oh dear! I do hope it isn't going to refuse the food now," Dan lamented.

"Try daubing the mixture on its whiskers again with the end of the baster," Grandpa suggested.

Dan gently rubbed the whiskers, squeezing some of the mixture over the seal's mouth. For a moment the seal hesitated, then licked at its mouth and its whiskers.

"At least it likes the mixture. Try again, Dan. Seals are

pretty intelligent. It may begin to link the baster with the idea of food. Press the bulb very gently, though."

Again Dan used the end of the baster to smear the seal's mouth with the mixture. This time the seal's reaction came quicker. It licked the sticky food off almost before Dan had finished rubbing it on its whiskers, and in doing so it gave a lick to the tube.

"Do that again, Dan," Grandpa directed. "I think we are getting somewhere. This time when the seal opens its mouth, put the tube in quickly and squirt some of the stuff down its throat."

Dan followed Grandpa's instructions. The moment the seal opened its mouth, he thrust in the tube and pressed the bulb. The seal pushed it out again!

"Oh dear, you silly little thing! Can't you see I'm trying to feed you?" Dan cried desperately.

"Patience, Dan! At least you got the tube inside its mouth and managed to squirt some food down its throat. We've just got to keep trying," Grandpa said. "Now, have another go."

Again Dan quickly advanced the tube when the seal opened its mouth and this time the seal did not put it out again. Dan squeezed the bulb quickly and the seal got a good mouthful of its food, but it seemed to have some difficulty in swallowing it.

Grandpa stroked the seal's throat quickly. "Its throat is dry for want of food. That's why it finds it hard to swallow," he said.

Once again he filled the baster with the mixture.

"It's got a fair bit down now. Keep on with the baster, Dan, and I'll massage its throat so it will swallow."

After several more attempts, at last the seal opened its mouth when Dan approached with the baster tube.

"It's getting the idea!" Dan cried.

It seemed as if the seal liked the feel of the oily mixture going down its throat. After a time, though, it began to tire.

"Well, that's more than half the flask of food down now," Grandpa announced with satisfaction. "There's still some left in the flask but we'll let the wee animal have a rest, then try it again. It seems to have got hold of the idea that the sight of the baster means food."

"Is it an *animal*, Grandpa?" Dan asked. "I thought it was a fish."

"Aye, Dan, all creatures that suckle their young, like mother-seals, are called *mammals*, and mammals are animals."

"What is it? A 'he' seal or a 'she' seal?" Dan wanted to know.

Grandpa shone the light from his lantern over the seal's fur.

"You can tell by the markings on its coat. Cow seals have quite light coats, almost white, with darker markings scattered over the fur here and there. Male seals have darker fur along the back but with a light marking on top of it. This seal's coat is practically completely white. I think she's a lady. She's not beginning to moult yet."

"What's 'moult'?" Dan looked up enquiringly.

"When a seal-calf is about a fortnight old, dark hairs appear at the edge of the flippers and on its muzzle. There are just one or two on this seal, faintly showing, so I judge it to be about a fortnight old." Grandpa Reid pointed to the marks. "Soon, at about three weeks, the calf begins to lose its first white coat and a darker coat shows underneath. The calf tries to rub off the first coat by scratching and rubbing itself against rocks. Sometimes, though, when a seal-pup has been starved, the moult is delayed. I think that is what has happened with this seal."

"Do you think it—*she*—will live, Grandpa?"

"Hard to tell, laddie, but we'll do our best to keep her alive."

"I'd like to give her a name," Dan said. "I've been calling her 'it' for so long."

"No harm in your giving her a name, though she may be a long time before she recognises it. What name have you in mind?"

Dan thought hard for a minute, then said, "I'm going to call her 'Grace' because seals are so graceful in the water when they swim and I hope she will swim some day."

Grandpa smiled at him. "A good name, especially if this seal came from the Farne Islands. There was a brave woman called Grace Darling, the lighthouse-keeper's daughter on the Farne Islands, who helped her father to save nine people from the wreck of the *Forfarshire* in a gale."

"I've heard about her at school," Dan said. "Do you think this seal came from the Farne Islands, Grandpa?"

"Most likely. There was a culling of the seals going on there over a week ago. Cow seals get alarmed at the shots and try to protect their calves. Maybe this one's mother was accidentally wounded, for the Norwegian cullers usually only shoot bull seals and not the mothers with calves. She probably plunged into the sea in fright and took her baby with her. Seals can swim when they are only a few days old. Their mothers teach them and help them. The mother sometimes swims underneath her calf and pushes it along with her back. I've watched them do that."

"But why did this seal's mother leave her here and not come back to her?" Dan asked.

"I think she was too badly wounded to make it as far as this shore, Dan. She managed to come as far as the Long Rig bank, and then she died. This baby seal was probably washed ashore by the tide, perhaps almost into the lime kiln itself, there was a very high tide at that time."

"And the baby seal waited for its mother and she never came?"

"That's right, Dan. Well, shall we have another shot at feeding Grace? There's quite a bit left in the flask."

This time the seal seemed to recognise the plastic end of the baster and to connect it with the good rich milk mixture she liked. She took the end in her mouth and did not spit it out so often, only when her mouth was full. At last she had swallowed the last of the food in the flask. Dan stroked her gently and she looked at him with large eyes, almost with a look of love.

"That'll have to do now till tomorrow morning," Grandpa said.

"But what *about* tomorrow morning?" Dan asked anxiously. "We've got no more tinned milk, have we?"

Grandpa chuckled. "I've got a friend at one of the hotels who will spare me a couple of tins till Kate arrives. And possibly Mrs Kerr can be persuaded to 'phone her supplier at Berwick to hasten a delivery. My! She'll be expecting your Grandma to produce a mountain of Scotch Tablet for the Church Sale!" He chuckled again. "Jings! We'd better be moving or your Grandma will give me the length of her tongue. Come on! Collect up these things and the lantern and let's get going."

Dan gave the seal a final stroke and said, "I'll be back at the first light, Grace."

As they left the kiln there came a plaintive bleating after them.

"That's a good sign," Grandpa said. "She doesn't want us to leave her. She's beginning to associate you with her supply of food. Maybe, in time she'll even think you're her mother!" Grandpa laughed.

As they jogged along over the beach Dan said, "I wish I'd told you about my seal at first, Grandpa."

"Well, it might have been better if you had done," Grandpa agreed. "But you tackled the job pretty well yourself."

"Grandpa, do you think Grandma's right when she talks about seals as if they were people?"

"Maybe, Dan lad, maybe! Your Grandma's a wise woman. She knows a lot about the lore of the sea. Some time soon we'll tell her about your seal, but right now, we'd better not vex her by being late for supper."

# 9      BRINGING UP A SEAL

The next morning Dan and Grandpa Reid were away to the lime kilns after a very hurried breakfast.

"What's got you both?" Grandma Reid wanted to know. "It's not nearly time for Aidan to go to school yet."

"It's just something Dan and I wanted to see to, together," Grandpa told her.

"If it isn't something to do with birds, it'll be something to do with fishes, I'll be bound," Dan's mother laughed.

"You might say that," Grandpa replied, smiling a little.

"Well, whatever it is, there's no call to be so mysterious about it," Grandma declared impatiently.

"Just see to it that you don't make that bairn late for school with your pranks and ploys, Dad," young Mrs Reid reminded him.

She watched them cross the shore towards the upturned boat-shed and come out with a bucket. "Now, I wonder what they're up to? Looking for bait?"

"Ah, well, it'll all come out in time," Grandma replied to Jenny Reid. "I'd better get busy with my baking, for Kate'll be home today."

Down at the lime kilns Dan played his signature tune. They were rewarded by an immediate answering quavering sound from the kiln.

"Grace sounds stronger," Dan cried gladly.

"At least she's recognised your music, Dan."

Grandpa had the milk and cod-liver oil mixture ready in the flask. He had been up early to prepare it in the ship's galley. He drew it up into the baster.

"Now, you lace Grace's whiskers with it. Don't bother with the spoon this time. Start right away with the baster tube and see if she's remembered the drill."

At first Grace drew her head back at the sight of the baster, but Dan held the end to her nose and let her sniff at it. She recognised the food smell and opened her mouth. Dan pushed the tube in at once and squirted some of the mixture down her throat.

"Gosh! Isn't she clever!" he exclaimed.

"Steady on!" Grandpa warned him. "Press the bulb gently and give her a little at a time. Don't choke her!"

When the contents of the baster were swallowed, Grace was quite ready for the next.

"Let's see if she'll let me massage her throat again this time," Grandpa suggested.

At his touch a look of surprise came into the seal's eyes. Grace gave a shiver but she did not draw back. She was accepting Grandpa too as part of the feeding-chain.

Soon every drop of food in the flask had been put into the baster and gently squirted down her throat.

"Now for the next move!" Grandpa said.

"The next? But she's finished all the milk mixture," Dan pointed out.

"True, but the next step is to give her a bath."

"A bath?" Dan was even more surprised.

"Yes. Touch her fur. Feel how dry and scaly it is. We've got to get her used to the feel of the salt water again."

Grandpa went to a rock pool and filled his bucket.

"Are you going to slosh it over her?" Dan asked, rather alarmed.

"No, no! Not at this stage. Gently does it."

Grandpa produced a large bath sponge from the bottom of his bucket. Then he squeezed it gently over Grace's back. She gave a little start of surprise, a slight shiver, but she did not even raise a protesting flipper. She shivered again when Grandpa squeezed the second spongeful over her, but this time it was more a shiver of delight. When he lifted the sponge for the third time she looked quite eagerly at him.

"That's what you were wanting, wasn't it, my lass? A good bath?" Grandpa said.

He continued squeezing the water all over her fur till the drops glistened. Then, when there was just about a pint of water left in the bucket, he said, "Now for the shower!" and lifted the bucket and emptied it over her.

Grace gave a happy bleating sound. There was no mistake. It was a cry of sheer delight.

"We must give her a bath every time we feed her until she's strong enough to go in the sea herself," he told Dan.

"In the sea?" Dan's voice quavered. "But—but won't she want to swim away then?"

Grandpa set down the bucket and looked at him. "Now, Dan, what do you want for your seal? Do you want her to stay on dry land where she'll die sooner or later, or to go back to the sea and learn to fend for herself?"

Dan looked troubled. "—I'd like to keep her for always but—but she's a seal person, isn't she? and seals belong to the sea."

"Yes, seals belong to the sea," Grandpa agreed.

"Then—then I'll have to let her go back when she's ready." Dan's voice faltered.

Grandpa gripped his shoulder. "That's a wise decision, Dan. But I don't think Grace'll ever forget you and the island. Seals have long memories. Right now, though, she'll be a while yet before she's ready to take to the sea. You'll have her to look after till she's much bigger and stronger."

Dan stroked and patted Grace with affection. To his surprise she suddenly raised a fore-flipper and patted his foot! Grandpa laughed out aloud. "That's what seals and their mothers do—pat each other lovingly. *She's* adopting *you*, Dan."

"She's—she's wonderful! She's really intelligent," Dan declared.

Grandpa chuckled. "You'd better learn a new tune for that mouth-organ, *Amazing Grace*." Grandpa picked up the bucket and flask. "But right now you'd better play yourself out with *The Bluebells of Scotland*."

Grace watched them go with big longing eyes from which the tears rolled, and she raised one flipper as if she would have liked to follow them.

When Kate arrived back on the island in the school bus that afternoon both Grandpa and Dan met her. She hauled a heavy canvas bag off the bus and Grandpa hurried to take it from her.

"Whew! That was heavy! Eight tins!" she exclaimed. "What on earth do you want with eight tins of condensed milk? Is Grandma starting a fudge factory?"

"Ssh! Not so loud!" Grandpa said. "It's a secret yet."

"But why did you want *two* jars of cod-liver oil too? And why did you both have to 'phone? And why couldn't Dan tell me what it was all about?"

"I'd used up all my coppers for the 'phone," Dan told her, "so I couldn't go on talking."

"And I've spent every penny I've got on tins of milk," Kate retorted.

"Now, listen, Kate! Please don't say a word about all those tins of condensed milk at home," Grandpa told her.

"Why? Not to Grandma even?"

"Not to anyone!" Grandpa said firmly. "After tea Dan

and I will let you into our secret. That's a promise. Meanwhile you can tell me what you've spent and I'll refund it."

Dan gave his grandfather a grateful look.

Grandpa carried the precious tins down to the shed on the shore.

At tea-time Kate kept her side of the bargain, but she did ask her grandmother rather curiously, "Are you making Scotch Tablet, Grandma?"

"No, my lassie, not yet. Strange, though! You're the second person to ask me that today. Mrs Kerr at the shop said, 'You're surely very busy making fudge'—that's what she called it—'for the Church Sale, Mrs Reid?' And when I told her I wasn't, she looked quite surprised. I wonder why?"

Nobody answered Grandma's question, but Grandpa and Dan exchanged furtive glances.

After tea Grandpa beckoned Kate and Dan out of the house and they followed him to the ship-store where he picked up the parcel of tins of condensed milk and the cod-liver oil and the big thermos flask. "Now we'll go down to the 'Jenny'," he announced.

"What are we going there for?" Kate wanted to know.

"You'll see when we get there," Grandpa said mysteriously. He led them up the gang-plank and down into the galley. There he emptied two tins of condensed milk into a pan with half a bottle of cod-liver oil and started the little calor gas stove to heat it up. Then he put half a pound of butter to melt in the mixture.

"Whatever's that horrible stuff for?" Kate asked.

Grandpa laughed as he stirred vigorously. "It's for a pet of Dan's. Hasn't he told you yet?"

"No."

"Well, he's got it over in the lime kilns."

Kate's mouth dropped open. "The lime kilns! What has he got there?"

"Wait till you see," Dan told her. "We're going there now."

"What? Why, it's almost dark!"

"We'll take the lantern and you'll see all right," Grandpa said.

Kate shivered. "I don't know if I'm all that keen to come."

"Oh, there's nothing to be afraid of," Dan assured her. "You'll love it when you see it."

Grandpa had been cooling down the mixture slightly. "There! That's just about right. Come on, both of you."

Kate's curiosity got the better of her, and the three of them scrambled over the rocky path round the Ouse to the lime kilns. Grandpa led the way with the lantern and Dan carried the bucket with the flask inside. As they approached the entrance Dan took his mouth-organ from his pocket and played the tune the seal knew. A plaintive wailing like a baby crying answered them immediately.

"Oh, what's that?" Kate cried. "You've surely not got a baby in there?"

"Yes, it's a baby," Dan chuckled. "But it's rather a large-sized baby. Come on, Kate! You'll love it."

The seal's eyes looked larger than ever and her white fur glistened in the lantern light. Kate's mouth fell open.

"Oh! Oh! It's a seal! It's beautiful. But why are you keeping it here?"

"I'm not *keeping* her. She got stranded here and we think her mother's dead." Dan launched into the tale of how he found the baby seal. "And now we're feeding her," he concluded. "That's why we needed the condensed milk—for Grace."

"Grace?"

"That's the name I've given her."

"We'd better get on with feeding," Grandpa said. "Now, you watch carefully what we do, Kate, for I'll probably be out on the boat on Monday and then Dan would need you to lend a hand."

When Dan produced the baster Kate let out a cry of surprise. "Oh, what would Grandma have to say to that?"

Grandpa looked slightly guilty, but he said, "We'll be telling her some time."

Halfway through Grace's meal, Kate said, "Can I have a go with the baster?"

Dan hesitated, but Grandpa said, "Yes, show Kate what to do, Dan. Grace had better get to know her."

"Squeeze the bulb gently and slowly, then," Dan said, just a bit reluctant to give it up.

When the meal was over Grandpa bathed Grace with the

sponge. The little seal lifted first one flipper and then the other in evident enjoyment.

"That's more movement than ever she's shown before," Dan declared, delighted.

"Yes, she's not as weak as she was. Tomorrow I think we'll try to introduce her to fish," Grandpa decided.

"Fish! But she won't be able to go fishing, will she?" Dan cried, astonished.

"Not yet! I mean we'll try to introduce a little fish in her diet."

"But we can't put fish in the baster tube."

"No. We'll have to try to think a way round that one."

The next day was Saturday.

"I'll meet you at the lime kilns," Grandpa whispered to Dan after breakfast.

"But the food?" Dan whispered back.

"I'll bring it along. Tell Kate, though, not to wear that red sweater she had on at breakfast but to put on a navy one instead."

Dan could not understand why Grandpa was so interested in Kate's appearance.

"Seals don't like bright colours. They frighten them," Grandpa hissed in Dan's ear.

Kate was surprised too, but she obeyed Grandpa's instruction.

When Grandpa joined them at the lime kilns he was carrying some fish at the bottom of his bucket. Grace took the milk, cod-liver oil and butter mixture from the baster tube with no hesitation.

"She really is clever," Dan said proudly.

"We'll see if she's as clever with the fish now," Grandpa said, offering Grace a herring. She sniffed at it but she did not open her mouth. Grandpa tried again but this time Grace determinedly turned her head on one side.

"Choosy, aren't you?" Grandpa said. "Let's try a small mackerel instead." But Grace would have none of the mackerel either.

"Now what are we going to do?" Grandpa said, scratching his head. "Milk and oil won't keep her alive for ever. She's going to have to learn to like fish, so she'll be encouraged soon to go fishing for herself."

"She's got to grow up, hasn't she?" Dan remarked sadly.

"If she won't take this fish from our hands, then we're going to have to thrust it in when she opens her mouth," Grandpa said. "It'll have to be pushed right in and I doubt if we should do that with our hands."

"Why not?" Dan said.

"She might snap her teeth shut on both fish *and* hand.

Although she's a baby, she's already got quite strong teeth. Maybe we could impale the fish on a pointed stick ... but she might break the point off and it could stick in her throat."

"I know what you could use," Kate said eagerly. "You could use a pair of tongs."

"That's an idea," Grandpa agreed, "but ordinary coal tongs are rather short, and besides, Grandma would miss them from the fireside."

"What about those long old-fashioned brass tongs inside the brass fender in the parlour?" Kate asked.

"Just the job! We'll bring them along with us this afternoon for Grace's second feed. I don't know if your grandmother would approve of it, though. She's very proud of her brass-ware." Grandpa looked doubtful. "Maybe *I'd* better be responsible for borrowing the tongs. I wouldn't like either of you to get into trouble."

That afternoon, just before darkness fell, Grandpa Reid with Dan and Kate set off along the harbour to the "Jenny". From the living-room Grandma and young Mrs Reid watched them walking round towards Steel End.

"What ploy are they up to now?" Grandma asked.

"My! but Dad is walking stiffly. He's got quite a limp," Jenny Reid said.

"He never said a word about his rheumatism though. That's queer!" Grandma remarked.

Little did she know that Grandpa had the long tongs slung from his waistband inside his trouser leg!

Once again Grace replied to Dan's mouth-organ with happy sounds. This time, as they entered the lime kilns, she rose slightly on her front flippers as though she was coming to greet them. She let Dan and Grandpa pat her, then Kate. It was clear that she was accepting Kate as a friend too. Then she lifted one flipper and tapped Dan's foot with it.

"I do believe she's *asking* for her food," Dan said, and hastened to fill the baster and put it to her mouth. She opened her mouth at once.

"Only give her the first half of the mixture, Dan," Grandpa instructed him as he retrieved the long tongs from his trouser leg. From the basket he carefully picked up a piece of mackerel with the tongs. "Before you put the rest of the mixture in the baster, I'll dip this in it." He dipped the fish and the end of the tongs into the mixture in the flask. "Now, make as if you are going to give her the baster again, but move it quickly away from her when she opens her mouth."

Dan did as he was instructed. When Grace opened her mouth to receive the baster, quick as thought Grandpa thrust in the tongs. Grace looked surprised and tried to push the tongs out, but Grandpa opened them slightly and the fish fell into the seal's mouth. Grace was certainly puzzled, but this new food tasted of the milk mixture into which it had been dipped. Then, by instinct, she chewed at it slightly and turned it over in her mouth.

"Quick, Dan! Massage her throat so she has to swallow it," Grandpa directed.

Gulping slightly, Grace swallowed the fish.

"Now some more milk mixture through the baster but not all of it," Grandpa ordered. "Stop halfway. Make her come after the baster with her mouth open and I'll slip the tongs in again."

Once more the trick worked and once more Grace swallowed the fish, Kate massaging her throat vigorously this time.

"This is what we'll have to do to get her used to a fish diet," Grandpa decided. "Heaven help me, though, when your Grandma finds out what I'm doing with her precious tongs!"

Grace watched them with sorrowful eyes as they packed up to leave her; then, when they gave her their goodbye pats, she lifted a flipper and patted Dan on the leg. As they turned away she hoisted herself on her fore-flippers and pushed her body forward a little way as though she would follow them.

"Jings! Did you see that?" Dan exclaimed.

"Aye. She made a move to come after us," Grandpa agreed.

"She couldn't have done that a few days ago. She's getting stronger," Dan said with satisfaction.

"That's true. Another few meals with the fish and we'll try enticing her out to a rock pool for her bath," Grandpa told them.

By the second meal on Sunday Grace was accepting the tongs and chewing at the fish with evident enjoyment, though she was still keen to have the milk mixture too. She even let Kate hold the baster in her mouth.

"The next move is to give her more of the fish and less of the milk," Grandpa decided. "Tomorrow, Monday, I'll have to go out in the boat with your father to put out the lobster pots, but on Tuesday morning we'll see if we can encourage Grace to move a bit further. When do you go back to school, Kate?"

"Wednesday evening, if the tide's right to let the bus cross the causeway."

"It will be," Grandpa said, doing a rapid calculation of the tide times. "Then tomorrow, Kate, will you help Dan to feed Grace?"

"Oh, yes! She'll take the baster from me too now," Kate said.

"You can operate the tongs then, Dan?" Grandpa asked.

"Oh, sure!"

"Then we'll leave them here. I'll leave plenty of fish for you in the basket too. Kate, do you think you could manage to heat the mixture just slightly?"

Kate giggled. "I'll wait till Grandma goes shopping," she said.

# IO TOM WATSON GETS A FRIGHT

Kate did indeed seize the opportunity to prepare the milk mixture when Grandma Reid went along to Mrs Kerr's shop, and she had just put the pans back on the shelf when Grandma returned. Old Mrs Reid was wearing a puzzled look.

"Mrs Kerr asked me again how I was getting on with the fudge-making," she said. "When I told her I hadn't started yet she looked surprised. That's the second time she's asked. This time she said, 'Oh, you're buying in the tins ready?' I didna' ken what she meant. Before I could ask her, Mrs Watson came in, so I just gathered up my shopping and came away. The woman seems obsessed wi' the notion o' my tablet-making."

"Dan and I have finished washing the breakfast dishes, Grandma." Kate hurriedly changed the subject.

"Have you made your beds?"

"Before we came down for breakfast," Kate assured her.

"Good bairns! Well, you can away out now and enjoy your holiday."

Dan and Kate flung on their anoraks and were out of the door in the twinkling of an eye. Kate snatched up the flask from where she had hidden it behind the door. The bucket with the fish had already been left by Grandpa in the lime kiln the night before, and the baster and the tongs had also been left there.

Grace greeted them with bleating barks of joy. She whined in a kind of tune to Dan's mouth-organ.

"She's singing!" Kate exclaimed.

"Grandma once told us seals could sing. I think she believes they are *people*, sea people. What do you think, Kate?"

"I'm not sure … Grandma knows a lot of things."

They set about feeding Grace. She took her milk mixture, then looked eagerly towards the bucket holding the fish. She even shifted her flippers a little and edged forward slightly.

"See that?" Dan exclaimed. "She likes the fish and she knows we keep it in that bucket. Now, isn't she clever?"

"I expect she can smell it. Grandpa said we were only to give her half the fish for breakfast and keep the rest for her evening meal," Kate reminded Dan. "He said he's bringing some more with him from the boat for tomorrow."

Grace had got used to the tongs now, too, and took the fish from them quite daintily into her mouth.

"She's getting fatter too," Dan announced with pride. "All those folds of skin round her neck are filling out."

"Dan, have you told anyone except Grandpa about your seal?" Kate asked suddenly.

"No. Why?"

"You haven't told Tom Watson?"

"He'd be the last person on earth I'd tell! He's a mean beast. What makes you ask about him?"

"Because when we came out of church yesterday he hedged up alongside me and muttered, 'See you at the lime kilns.'"

"I hate him! He's cruel to birds and animals." Dan told Kate about the fulmar petrels.

"He's a right coward, really," Kate said thoughtfully. "He only picks on creatures and people who can't hit back at him. Don't worry, Dan! If he comes back here I think we'd be a match for him."

"Yes, but on Wednesday you go back to school," Dan reminded her. "And if Tom Watson comes to the kilns when Grandpa and I are not here and he finds Grace, what will he do to her? She's still not big enough to fight him and she couldn't get away if he threw stones at her."

"There are ways of dealing with Tom Watson without fighting him," Kate said with an air of mystery.

They put the bucket and tongs beside Grace as they prepared to go. Grace looked after them sadly and, as they left, she raised herself on her flippers and followed them for more than a metre.

"Go back, Grace! We'll be here again this evening." Dan called to her. On the way home he said, "It'll be rather dark when we've finished feeding her after tea. You—you won't mind coming down here then, Kate?"

"No. There'll be the two of us. It's a pity Grandpa couldn't leave us the lantern, but he'll need it on the 'Jenny'," Kate said.

That afternoon Grandma went to visit an old friend. Before she left she asked Kate to take a knitting-pattern to Mrs Kirk in Marygate. "Don't go till near on tea-time. She'll be at her daughter's till late on in the afternoon," Grandma told Kate.

After Grandma had gone, Kate took the opportunity to make the milk mixture. Without thinking, she then put the empty tins and the cod-liver oil jar into the dust bin. The late afternoon sun began to sink over Fenham Flats and it was time for Dan and Kate to go to feed Grace.

"Oh, bother! I nearly forgot to take the pattern to Mrs Kirk," Kate exclaimed. "You go along by the shore road,

Dan, and I'll come over from Marygate by the Castle Path to the lime kilns and join you there."

"All right!" Dan agreed.

As Dan went along by the shore path he was unaware that he was watched by Tom Watson from his house near the Popple Well. "Now, what are you doing over at the lime kilns, Dan Reid?" Tom Watson muttered to himself. "I've a good mind to go and see."

Just then Tom's mother called him, "Come and get your tea, Tom."

Tom swallowed down his tea as fast as he could, but the delay held him back a while and Dan reached the lime kilns safely. Soon afterwards, Kate came along the top path just below the Castle, and unseen by Tom Watson who was still at his tea, she joined Dan just as he was getting out his mouth-organ to play his signature tune.

A joyful sound from Grace answered Dan's tune. Poised on her flippers, the little seal shuffled forward to meet them. An overturned bucket lay beside her. Dan picked it up. It was empty!

Kate looked at Grace. The seal gave a sneaking lick to her whiskers. She had a look of smug satisfaction.

"I do believe she's eaten them!" Kate cried. She examined the fur on the top of Grace's head. "Yes, she has! There are fish scales on her fur—do you see? She must have dipped her head in the bucket and upset it and got the fish out. Now, I call that real clever!"

"That way it won't be long before she can feed herself," Dan said a little sadly. Once Grace became independent she would not need him any more.

"Well, that saves us the bother of handing her the fish with the tongs tonight. We'll be able to take them back to the parlour before Grandma misses them. We'll just give Grace the milk mixture now," Kate decided.

They had just finished feeding Grace and were putting the tongs and flask ready to take away when they heard a sound from the pathway by the rocks. Someone was playing a portable radio. Dan gripped Kate by the forearm. "That's Tom Watson coming. It couldn't be anyone else."

Dan put his head out of the lime kiln. Silhouetted against the setting sun, though still at a distance, Tom Watson was approaching, his radio blaring away.

"Listen, Dan, and do just what I say!" Kate said urgently. "Tom Watson doesn't know that I'm here. He'll think you're alone. I'm going to nip out round the corner and on to the top of the lime kilns."

"What good will that do?" Dan asked.

"The old vents—the chimneys, you know—go right down into the lime kilns. I'm going to scare Tom Watson. Now *you* must lure him past Grace's hiding place and round the corner and into the entrance of one of the other kilns there. Whatever you do, don't let him know that I'm up above. And don't be frightened yourself, no matter what happens. I'm off!" Kate snatched up the bucket, and, keeping close to the side of the kilns, she dodged round the corner and up the slope. Tom Watson, intent on picking his way over the rocky path, did not see her dark little figure disappear round the corner of the lime kilns.

Kate quickly reached the steps that led over the high wall surrounding the lime kiln. By the steps was the notice board which warned visitors to the island that the area round the top of the lime kilns was not safe, and that children or dogs must not venture there alone, as the vents were still open. Kate, however, knew her way well among the open shafts. She crouched down by the centre shaft of one of the side kilns and waited, her bucket beside her. She was not visible from the rocky path along the beach. The sound of Tom Watson's radio drowned any noise she made as she scrabbled up handfuls of loose old ashes that still lay crumbled beside the vents, and dropped them in the bucket.

Below the front kilns Dan waited, shivering a little, till his enemy was in sight. He moved well away from the kiln where Grace was hidden and prayed that she would not make a sound. He stood by the far corner of the kilns till Tom Watson saw him.

"Hi, young Reid! What are you up to over there?"

"Mind your own business!" Dan shouted back boldly, though his voice quavered a little. He dodged away round the corner of the kilns, and Tom Watson came running after him.

"What are you hiding here?" Tom demanded.

For answer Dan stood defensively in front of the entrance to the middle kiln along the side path. At least Tom Watson had passed the front kilns where Grace was hidden. It was his business to lure Tom Watson into one of the side kilns now, as Kate had told him to do.

"You're not to go in there!" he told Tom Watson, knowing full well that this was just what would make Tom go into the kiln.

"Who says I've not to?" Watson jeered.

"It . . . it's *haunted*!" Dan said desperately. "I wouldn't go in there for anything!"

"You!" Tom Watson cried contemptuously. "You're just a silly frightened baby! I don't believe you! You're trying to hide something in there. I'm going in and you're going in with me!"

"No, no!" Dan cried, pretending to resist.

"Yes, you are!" Tom Watson took a firmer grip on Dan's jersey and lugged him in after him. Dan pretended to struggle till Tom Watson was right under the vent, then with a shout of "Let me go!" he tore himself free.

Before Tom Watson could swing round and catch hold

of him again there came an eldritch screech and a horrible cackle of laughter that echoed down the vent. It was followed by a clattering shower of old ashes that fell upon Tom Watson from above as Kate emptied the bucket down the shaft. Tom gave a terrified shriek and, half-blinded by the ash dust, he pushed past Dan and fled though the entrance. As he rushed towards the shore, he caught his foot in a hole beside a boulder and went crashing to the ground. For a moment he lay there winded, then he tried to get up again. He sank back again clutching at his ankle. "Oh, my foot! My foot!" he yelled.

Dan saw his enemy fall, and he stopped at the kiln entrance not knowing what to do.

"Help me! Help me! I can't get up!" Tom Watson cried.

Dan hesitated. Was this just a trick on Tom Watson's part? If he stooped over him, would Tom Watson attack him? Just then Kate came down from the path above. "What happened?" she wanted to know.

"Tom Watson was running away and he tripped up and fell. He says he can't get up."

"Maybe he's just pretending," Kate said.

"What if he's not? We...we can't just leave him lying there and the tide coming in, can we?"

Again there came a wail from Tom Watson. "Dan Reid, come and help me! Don't leave me!" His voice sounded desperate.

"We'll have to do something," Dan declared, fearful but determined.

"Yes," Kate agreed. "He can't very well tackle both of us at once."

They ran towards Tom Watson. "Get up, Tom Watson! You silly idiot!" Kate shouted.

"I...I can't! I can't stand. It's my ankle. I think it's broken," Tom Watson almost wept. "Help me!"

"I'll take this side of him. You take the other, Dan," Kate directed. "Now, sit up, Tom Watson!"

"It's you, Kate!" Tom gasped, astonished.

"Yes, it's *me*," Kate answered grimly. "Now, put one arm round my neck and the other round Dan's and when I say 'Heave!' stand up on your good leg."

"I . . . I don't know if I can!" Tom faltered.

"Oh, yes, you can!" Kate told him. 'Hook on as you've been told."

Without further argument Tom Watson "hooked on".

"Heave!" Kate ordered, and with her arm and Dan's linked behind Tom Watson's back they both heaved hard. Tom planted his good foot firmly on the ground and heaved too. There he stood like a stork on one leg.

"Now we've got to get you home," Kate said. "Can you walk at all?"

Tom Watson tried his injured ankle on the ground and sharply drew it up again with a yelp of pain.

"Walking's no use," Dan declared. "Can you hop if we hold you up?"

Tom attempted to hop with their aid and managed a few metres towards the path.

"We can't take him along the shore," Dan said to Kate. "There are too many slippery rocks that way."

"No, it'll have to be by the top path," Kate agreed. "But how shall we get him up the steep sloping bit?"

"Can you manage to crawl a few yards on hands and knees?" Dan asked Tom.

"I'll try."

"Once we're up the slope we'll lift you again," Kate told him.

Wincing with pain Tom managed to haul himself on hands and knees up the steep slope to where the path began to level out beside the big wall surrounding the kiln top.

"He'll never manage to hop all that way home," Dan said. "Let's try carrying him on our hands the way I saw the fisherman bring Willie Cobbett up the ramp when he fell and broke his leg."

"How?" Kate asked.

"We link our hands like we did before but Tom sits on them with his arms round our necks and we carry him."

Once more they heaved Tom into position and set off along the path which wound downhill to the village. It took them a long time with many rests, but at last they reached the door of Tom's house. They propped him against the wall and Dan knocked hard at the door. It was opened by Mrs Watson.

"What on earth...!" she exclaimed.

"Tom's had a fall and hurt his ankle," Kate explained, her breath coming fast.

"You silly lad! Come inside!" Mrs Watson exclaimed.

"I...I can't walk, Ma," Tom told her in a quavering voice. It was then Mrs Watson noticed by the light streaming from the passage that Tom was very pale.

"Fred! Fred, come here!" she shouted over her shoulder. "Tom's hurt!"

Fred Watson came running. "What's wrong?"

"Tom fell and hurt his ankle," Kate explained again.

Mr Watson picked Tom up and carried him into the living-room, set him on the settee and began to strip off Tom's shoe and stocking. Already the ankle was very swollen.

"Where did this happen?" he asked.

"Down by the old lime kilns," Dan began to explain truthfully when he was interrupted by Mrs Watson.

"What were you doing down there?"

Tom looked helplessly at Dan and Kate but fortunately Mrs Watson went on without waiting for an answer. "How often have I told you not to go playing round there, Tom?"

Kate suddenly found her voice. "I guess we shan't be *playing* round there again now we've got Tom home. Maybe we should be going home too. It's dark and our folk will be wondering where we've got to."

As she and Dan turned towards the door, Tom mumbled, "Thanks. Thanks a lot ... for everything." Kate and Dan knew by this that Tom was grateful, too, that they had not told his parents what he was really up to at the lime kilns.

On the way home Dan said, "Kate, I never knew that you could screech like that. You sounded just like a witch."

"I learned that at school," Kate told him.

"What? To shriek like a witch? They never teach things like that at the school?"

"Oh, yes!" Kate laughed at his surprise. "I told you I was a witch in the school play and the teacher taught me how to give a screech and a cackling laugh. Anyway, it fair scared Tom Watson."

"I didn't know you did things like that at school," Dan said thoughtfully.

"Oh, yes! We do other things too, like playing table-tennis at the hostel, and we have sing-songs. I'm learning to play chess too. It's really quite jolly."

"But don't you miss the island, Kate?"

"Well, of course I do, but there's no time to get homesick, and anyway, we come home every week-end."

Dan nodded. He turned over in his mind what Kate had said and somehow the school on the mainland no longer seemed such a bleak prospect.

"I wonder if Tom Watson has really broken his ankle?" he said.

"I'll call round and enquire tomorrow," Kate said.

Next afternoon Kate did knock at the Watsons' door and ask about Tom.

"We've had the doctor to him," Mrs Watson told her. "The ankle's not broken but it's badly sprained and he'll not be at school for a week."

Kate took this news to Dan. "It doesn't look as if Tom Watson will be bothering you at the lime kilns for a while yet, so Grace will be safe from him."

"She'll have the chance to grow strong now. I'm a bit sorry for Tom Watson, for all that," Dan said.

At the cottage Grandma and their mother were already cooking supper ready for the return of their father and Grandpa from the fishing. Grandma was very quiet and had little to say. She did not even ask them where they had been.

That night, after everyone else had gone to bed, Grandma looked at Grandpa as he smoked his last pipe by the fire, "I think there's a bit of explaining to be done, James."

"What about, lass?"

"Weel, I had occasion to put out some potato peelings in the dustbin and I found some gey queer things in it."

"Such as what?"

"Twa-three empty condensed milk tins and a jar with a cod-liver oil label on it."

Grandpa stared at her nonplussed.

"How did *they* get there, James?"

"Er—*I* didn't put them there," Grandpa began, but Grandma looked at him with a steely eye over her knitting.

"Maybe no', but you'll ken who put them there, James. Was it Kate or Aidan?"

"Maybe, maybe," was all Grandpa could say.

"Weel, whether they did or they didna', condensed milk and cod-liver oil take money to buy and those children havena' pocket money enough for that. Besides, Mrs Kerr dropped in to Nelly Thomson's just before I left and she asked again about my tablet-making, so I just speired at her why she wanted to know."

Grandpa stopped smoking and stared at Grandma, at a loss what to reply.

"It was then she told me about all the condensed milk and cod-liver oil that you and Aidan had been buying and how she'd had to order more from the mainland," Grandma went on.

"And what did you tell her?" Grandpa asked.

"Nothing, for I didna' know. I just said it was something to do with some fishing ploy you had, maybe, and she had to be content wi' that. But *now* you can tell me what it is, James."

Grandpa drew a long breath. "I meant to tell you some time, Mary, but I'd promised Dan to keep it a secret."

"Oh, so you and Aidan have a secret between you? Has it something to do with the lime kilns?"

Grandpa nodded unhappily.

"Then you're keeping some creature there that has to be fed on condensed milk and cod-liver oil?"

"How did you know?" Grandpa asked.

"It takes no Master Mind to put two and two together to make four. D'ye think I've no eyes in my head? I've seen you and Aidan traipsing over the rocks towards the lime kilns and you canna' hide a bucket up your sleeve. That and the condensed milk gave me a clue. And then Kate and Aidan went off that way by themselves today."

"You notice a lot, lass!" Grandpa had to laugh.

"Weel, what kind of a creature is it. No, don't tell me! I'll make a guess. It's a seal!"

"Well, yes it is," Grandpa admitted. "You're a clever woman, Mary."

"Ah, well, maybe I am, but flattery will get you nowhere. But what I canna' understand is why you had to take my best pair of brass tongs oot o' the parlour?"

Grandpa gasped. "So you found that out too?"

"You forget I give the brass fender and the fire-irons a polish every week. Did ye think I'd no' miss the tongs? What for did you want them?"

"To feed the fish to the seal," Grandpa confessed. "They came in fine and handy for putting the fish in her mouth."

A slight smile curled round Grandma Reid's mouth. "'Her'? So the seal's a cow, eh?"

"A very small cow yet," Grandpa explained. "Dan found her abandoned in the lime kilns. She's just a baby. We think her mother was wounded in the culling on the Farnes. Maybe it was accidental, but a seal's body was seen on the Long Rig Bank. We think she was bringing her baby to take refuge on Lindisfarne but died before she got here, and the high tide brought the baby ashore."

A look of pity overswept Grandma's face. "The poor wee creature!" she whispered.

"Aye, she was near dying of hunger when Dan found her."

"Why couldna' Aidan have told me about her? He kens fine I love the seals." Grandma sounded hurt.

"He didn't exactly tell *me*." Grandpa went on to explain about the fight he had interrupted between Dan and Tom Watson and how when Dan played his mouth-organ the seal had replied from the lime kiln.

"Weel, surely you needn't have kept it a secret from me, James?" Grandma's voice still sounded hurt.

"I ought to have let you into the secret," Grandpa admitted. "But you see, Mary, it was *Dan's* secret and I'd promised to keep it. I think he was afraid he might be stopped from feeding his little seal."

"Aidan should have known me better than that. Have I no' told him about the seals in Shetland when I was a bit lassie? What else can I do to make him trust me?" Grandma sounded rather upset.

"In his heart I'm sure he trusts you," Grandpa reassured

her. "But times you talk to him a wee bit stiff, Mary my dear. Maybe you should try calling him Dan like I do, instead of Aidan."

Grandma stared at him. "I had no idea that he—he—" she broke off. "My, but bairns are queer kittle-kattle!"

Breakfast next morning was over, Dan's father had gone down to the "Jenny" to load lobster pots and his mother had departed to the mead factory, when Grandpa said, "Well, are you ready, Dan and Kate?"

Quietly Grandma Reid set an unopened tin of condensed milk on the table beside Dan. "Maybe you could make use of that?"

Dan's eyes met his grandmother's in astonishment. She was smiling at him! "You—you *know*?" Dan gasped.

She nodded. "I'm no' blind, laddie!"

Suddenly Dan leaped to his feet and rushed round the table to her. His arms went round her in a bear-like hug. "Oh, Grandma! Grandma! I'm *glad* you know!" he cried.

"Steady now! Dinna' choke me!" Grandma laughed. "Maybe I'll get coming to have a look at your seal some time, eh, Dan?"

"Oh, yes! Yes!"

It was not till Dan was walking along beside Grandpa and Kate towards the lime kilns that he realised what had happened. "Grandma called me *Dan*!" he exclaimed.

"Aye, she called you Dan," Grandpa repeated in a voice of quiet satisfaction.

Grace greeted Dan's refrain with her musical bleating. To their surprise she had hauled herself forward almost to the entrance of the kiln on their approach.

"Look at her! She can move about!" Dan cried.

"She's certainly gained in strength since two days ago," Grandpa agreed. "Let's give her the milk mixture and see what happens after that."

Grace opened her mouth eagerly for the baster tube and took the milk down with great swallowing sounds and evident enjoyment, but all the time her eyes kept straying towards the bucket which held the fish.

"Ah, you know what's in there, don't you, lassie?" Grandpa stroked her back.

"Oh, Grandpa, we haven't got the tongs," Kate cried. "Shall I go and beg the loan of them from Grandma?"

"No need for that, Kate. If Grace could take the fish out of the bucket when we were not there, she can manage without the tongs now."

"Are you going to give her the bucket then?"

"No. It's time now for her next lesson." Grandpa took a fish out of the bucket and offered it to Grace with his hand. To their surprise she took it eagerly but quite gently, without even snatching at his fingers.

"You have a go now, Dan. Hold the fish well back at the tail and offer her the head first. Let go of the fish as soon as she opens her teeth for it."

Dan felt rather tense as he held the fish. Suppose Grace snapped at it and his hand too? But Grace took the fish as gently as before.

"She's got manners," Kate said with approval.

"Now we'll try the next move," Grandpa decided. He took another fish and put it down on the kiln floor a couple of metres in front of Grace. Grace eyed it but made no move, though her nose twitched.

"Come and get it, Grace," Grandpa encouraged her, moving the fish a foot nearer to her. "Keep very still, Dan and Kate. Don't distract her."

Nothing happened for the next two or three minutes, but Grace kept her eyes fixed hungrily on the fish. Once her mouth opened and a tiny trickle of saliva escaped. Then, all at once, it was as though she made up her mind. She heaved

herself up on her fore-flippers, then launched herself forward.
Now she was less than a metre from the tempting fish. She
sniffed the air, and her nose and whiskers twitched again.
Then once more she made a sudden thrust forward of her
round body, put out a flipper and drew the fish close to her.
A quick gulp and it was gone! Dan and Kate jumped for
joy. "Well done, Grace!" Dan cried.

"Quiet, you two!" Grandpa cried in a low warning voice.
"The lesson isn't over yet." He looked behind him. "A good
thing it's high tide!" The waves were spilling over into a
nearby rock pool. Grandpa laid a trail of three herring towards the pool. "Come on, Grace!" he said, touching the
first fish.

Hesitantly at first, stopping often to stare about her, Grace
hauled herself over the mouth of the cave to the first fish.

That went down her throat too. Slowly she advanced on the next two, and looked round at Dan as if for help, but when he made no move, she swallowed those herring in turn too. Then Grandpa dropped the last herring in the rock pool.

Grace leaned forward over the pool, looking at the fish lying on the bottom a little way from the edge. She tried to reach it with her flipper and gave quite a start of surprise when her flipper came out wet with salt water. She tried with the other flipper but the fish was still too far for her to reach. She looked up appealingly at Grandpa.

"No, Grace! If you want it, you must go in and get it for yourself," he told her.

The splashing of a little wave in the pool made the fish seem to stir for a moment. Grace looked at the fish with large eyes, then instinct played a part. Fearful of losing the fish, she launched herself head first into the pool. When she surfaced, she had the fish triumphantly between her jaws. She gave it a little toss, then swallowed it.

"Well done, Grace!" Grandpa cried this time. "No more tongs and buckets for you! In future you take your fish from the water."

All at once it seemed as if Grace had discovered the joy of the sea-water. She submerged again, letting it roll over her, then came up and shook the sparkling drops from her head joyfully. She came out of the rock pool, then turned in her clumsy waddling fashion on land and went into the pool again.

"No more sponge baths for you, Grace!" Grandpa laughed. "You've found your own salt-water bath!"

Dan looked rather troubled. "Will Grace be going in the sea next, Grandpa?"

"Very soon, I hope, but it may take a few days to get her used to the salt pools and we'll still have to bring fish for her."

"If she goes into the sea, perhaps she'll swim away altogether?" Dan said unhappily.

Grandpa looked at him with sympathy. He understood how fond Dan had become of his seal.

"Some day, Dan, Grace will have to take to the sea again if she's to live a seal's life. The amount of fish we can give her will not be enough for her as she grows bigger. Besides, some day she must join her own people, the seals, and become one of them."

"Like the seal-woman in Grandma's story?"

Grandpa gave him a quick warm look. "If that's the way you see it, Dan. But seals have long memories. I don't think she'll ever forget you."

"If she goes away, will she come back to the island again?"

"That I can't tell you, but she may do, for seals stay close to the place where they have been brought up. If she does, she will remember you and your music. And now we've got to get her back to the lime kiln for her own safety till she's grown bigger and stronger yet. You play your music and I'll wave this herring before her. I've kept one back on purpose."

Dan played and Grace came half out of the pool. Grandpa enticed her with the remaining fish and she followed him, raising herself on her flippers and heaving herself awkwardly forward in an attempt to close the distance between herself and the coveted herring. At last they reached the lime kiln. She stopped and sniffed suspiciously at first, then she realised it was a familiar place and she plunged in after Grandpa, who rewarded her at once with the herring.

"Grandpa, you should train seals for the circus," Kate said in admiration.

"No, Kate!" Grandpa said firmly. "I'd never do that. These creatures have a right to their own place, and that's the sea."

The tide was already on the turn as they went back to the cottage. The children who went to school on the main-

land had to go back there when the tide was low enough
to leave the causeway dry so that the school bus could cross
to the mainland. They would be having their supper at the
hostel, St Aidan's. These arrangements always had to be
made to suit the tide. The family went to see Kate off on
the bus. This time Kate was regretful at leaving.

"Will Grace still be here when I come back on Friday?"
she asked her grandfather.

"I hope so, Kate. After all, it's only two days away."

The school bus was standing at Cambridge Corner.
Several children had already boarded it. Kate's father
handed up her suitcase to her. "See you next Friday, lassie."

"Don't forget to change your shoes and stockings if they
get wet," her mother reminded her. "And did you put that
new cake of soap in your wash-bag?"

"Yes, I remembered."

"Goodbye, Kate. There's nae need to bring back condensed milk this time," Grandma laughed.

The driver revved up his bus and Kate took her seat, then
the bus was away on the long macadam ribbon of road.

"Not long before you'll be joining Kate on the bus, Dan,"
his mother said a little sadly as they turned away.

"Aye, Jenny, they grow up that fast," Grandma remarked
with kind understanding.

# I I

## GRACE COMPLETES HER EDUCATION

On Friday, when Kate returned, the seal was still at the lime kiln. Grandpa Reid managed to go with Dan the next day, but on the following days he had to go fishing. Then Grandma Reid donned her thick tweed coat and headscarf and went along with Dan too. They had cut down the milk mixture considerably and increased the number of fish in Grace's diet.

"If Grace was still with her mother she would be almost weaned by now and learning to catch her own fish," Grandpa told Dan.

"That would mean she had to go into the sea?"

"Yes, Dan. It's got to come. We'll try her in the sea on Saturday afternoon when Kate's here and the tide will be high," Grandpa decided. "We'll start by putting more of her fish in the rock pool, except one which I'll keep to tempt her back to the kiln."

Grace was beginning to lose interest in the baster and milk and to watch eagerly for the fish trail to be put down to the pool. Each feeding time James Reid or Dan put the fish a little further away from her. Though she gave a bark or two in protest, she always flopped along to it in the end and then finally into the pool. She really enjoyed the pool and splashed in and out of it like a child in the sea. When Grandpa or Dan waved the last fish before her nose she always left the pool and came after it.

"Let's try a new game, Dan," Grandpa said. "Put the fish in the pocket of your anorak and let the head stick out. Play your tune and see if she'll follow you and take the fish."

Grace seemed quite puzzled when she saw Dan put the fish in his pocket, but she followed him, giving her bleating whine to accompany the music. Dan stopped as soon as he was under the archway to the kiln. She caught up with him and lifted her flippers up and down in a pleading way, keeping her eyes on the fish-head poking out of his pocket.

"Shall I give it to her?" Dan asked.

"Not yet! Point to it and pull it out a bit further and let's see what happens," Grandpa directed.

Suddenly it seemed as if Grace got the message. She leaped up, standing on her back-flippers, and snatched the fish from Dan's pocket.

"My! She's quick to learn," Grandpa declared. "From now on *you* must always keep a fish for her in your pocket, Dan. But soon she'll have to learn to catch her own fish."

"How do baby seals usually learn?" Dan wanted to know.

"Their mothers teach them when they start swimming in the sea. We'll just have to see what *we* can do about teaching her."

On Friday evening Kate arrived home again and was eager to go with them to see Grace on Saturday morning.

"Both of you put on your wellingtons this morning," Grandpa ordered as he put on his sea-boots.

"Now, James, take care!" Grandma warned him. "Don't be letting those bairns come home soaking wet or I'll have something to say to you."

"I'll take heed," Grandpa promised. "But what about you putting on your wellies and coming too, Mary?"

"Michty me! What will you be saying next?" Grandma cried, but she added, "Bide a wee, while I lift my boots from the cupboard. I may as weel come. That seal looks on me as one of the family now."

So all four of them set off for Castle Point.

At the lime kilns Grandpa handed each of them a fish. "No milk mixture today, just mackerel," he announced.

Already the tide was well up and close to the lime kilns.

"Kate, I want you and Grandma to show your fish to Grace and then paddle into the sea at the edge of the waves and drop your fishes there. Dan and I will wade just a bit further out with our fishes."

"Now, James, remember what I said," Grandma cautioned him.

Dan played his tunes and added a bar of *Amazing Grace* which he had been practising. Grandpa laid the trail by dropping one fish between the kiln archway and the sea. Grace emerged, shuffling her flippers and hauling her body awkwardly over the shingle.

"She's got a lot fatter in the last three days," Kate remarked.

"She's a lot stronger too," Grandpa agreed. "Come on, Grace, and get your fish."

Dan touched the mackerel with the toe of his boot. The fulmar petrels watched enviously. Grace waddled up to Dan and looked at him with her lovely liquid eyes.

"Go on, Grace! It's yours," Dan urged her.

Something of the great kindness in Dan's voice must have got through to her, for she lifted a flipper and patted Dan's boot, then she picked up the mackerel between her teeth and swallowed it whole. Dan walked towards Kate and Grandma. In turn they each dropped their fish where the incurving wave could just wash over the mackerel and appear to make them move. Grace did not hesitate. She wobbled forward and seized each fish in turn.

Grace splashed about happily at the edge of the incoming tide for a few minutes, then Grandpa, a few steps away in the sea, called Dan to come and stand by him. The sea came almost to the top of Dan's boots.

"Play your tune, Dan!"

Dan played a tune and Grace started to move towards him. Grandpa held up his fish so Grace could see it, then he flung it a couple of metres ahead in the water. She went after it and all at once she was water-borne and instinctively began to use her flippers and tail to take her through the water.

"She's *swimming*!" Kate cried.

Grace swallowed the fish, then, delighting in her new-found powers, she swept in a graceful curve round Grandpa and Dan.

"Oh, dear! Is she going out to sea?" Dan cried in a panic-stricken voice.

"Not yet, I think! Play her tune, Dan, and if she looks towards you, then show her your fish and see if she's persuaded to follow you."

The strains of *The Bluebells of Scotland* reached the seal. She paused in her second circuit of the bay and floated, rearing her head above the water and watching Dan inquisitively.

"See her!" Grandma laughed. "All seals are curious."

Grace swam lazily towards Dan. Dan held up his fish. Grace saw it and came plunging towards him. Dan turned and headed towards the lime kilns, Grace followed, wallowing clumsily in the shallows when her body touched the sand. Dan tucked the fish into the pocket of his anorak, letting Grace see where it was. She remembered the drill she had learned the past few days and waddled after him into the lime kiln. Then, quite gently, she pulled the fish from his pocket. Kate watched, amazed, but Grandma had something to say. "Now I know why Dan's clothes always smell of fish!" she scolded. "Mercy me! What'll you teach the lad next, James?"

Grace took up her usual position inside the lime kiln.

"She'll not stay there long now she's learned what she can do in the sea," Grandpa said. "She was in her element swimming around. We shan't be able to keep her out of it now."

For the next two or three days, however, Grace was content for them to feed the fish to her in the sea, but each day Dan noticed that she ventured out a little further into the Ouse Bay. She always returned, though, when he played the tune on his mouth-organ, and followed him to take the fish from his pocket. Then there came a day when Grace ventured further still into deeper water. Suddenly she saw a shadow swimming below her. Like lightning she dived towards it and pursued it through the water till she was near enough to grab it with her mouth. Triumphantly she surfaced, holding the fish up as if she wanted Grandpa and Dan to see it, then gave it a little toss in the air and swallowed it head-first.

"There! She's caught her first fish," Grandpa exclaimed. "The dead fish we give her will never taste as good now as the one she caught for herself. We can't hold her back now, Dan. She'll want to do her own fishing."

"I suppose she will," Dan said in a sad little voice.

For several days, though, Grace was still in the lime kiln when they visited her, though Dan noticed that she did not seem as eager or as hungry for the fish they took to her as she used to be.

"I think she's going into the water now when the tide reaches the lime kilns and catching her own fish," Grandpa said. "Look! There's the track of her body over the shingle— *two* tracks, one down to the water and one she made when she came back again."

"But she *did* come back," Dan pointed out hopefully.

"Some day, though, the urge will be on her to seek out her own folk," Grandpa warned Dan, and Dan knew he spoke the truth.

Then there came a day when the lime kiln was empty.

"She's gone!" Dan cried, his voice sharp with sorrow.

"Aye, but she's still in the bay." Grandpa pointed over the crest of the incoming wave where a grey head bobbed up and down. "There she is, sporting in and out of the waves. Play her tune, Dan, and see what she does."

Grace heard the music and reared up in the water in the upright position that seals can adopt when they are floating

and want to look round them. She spotted Dan and Grandpa
on the shore, sang her wavering discordant song and came
swimming towards them. When she reached the shore she
flopped and gambolled clumsily about them, evidently delighted to see them. Soon she found the fish in Dan's pocket,
and gently tapped his foot in affection with her flipper.

"Though she may not stay on the island now, I think
if she's in the sea nearby and hears you playing, Dan,
she'll come out of the sea to you. She's grown fond of
you."

"I've grown fond of her too," Dan said with a choke in
his voice.

Two or three days went by when Grace was not in the
kiln and there was no sign of her at all. Grandma noticed
Dan's stricken face. She felt she did not care how many fishy
anoraks and jeans she washed if the joy would come back
to Dan's face again, and she tried to comfort him.

"I think Grace'll still come back to see you now and again,
Dan. Seals are faithful people."

Dan noticed that, all unconsciously, Grandma had used
the word "people" for seals.

"Keep practising your mouth-organ down by the Ouse
and the lime kilns. She'll not forget your music, Dan."

Dan gave her a loving hug. He and Grandma had reached
a warm understanding over the seal and they had grown very
close to each other.

Faithfully each day Dan fetched a fish from the "Jenny"
and wandered along the shore playing all the tunes he knew,
but there was never a sign of Grace. Dan still went to the
lime kilns to look for her, though.

Then, one day, as he reached Castle Point by the shore
road, his enemy Tom Watson came limping round the corner
of the lime kilns from the upper path. Tom's ankle was still
bandaged but his curiosity had got the better of him and

he had decided to have another look inside the lime kilns by daylight. He was a bit taken aback to find Dan already there playing his mouth-organ.

"Still playing that thing?" he remarked. "Haven't you got a transistor yet?"

Dan was facing out to sea. Suddenly he saw a grey head bobbing up and down where the Ouse curved into deeper water. Defiantly he put the mouth-organ to his mouth and broke into *Amazing Grace*. The bobbing grey head came nearer.

"I can do better than that!" Tom Watson boasted and turned up the volume of his transistor radio. Just at that moment the "pop" programme ended and the sound faded away.

Out of the corner of his eye Dan saw the seal rapidly approaching the shore.

"I bet you can't do this with your stupid transistor!" he shouted, then burst as loud as he possibly could into *Amazing Grace* again.

Grace's bulky body came heaving through the shallow water. Tom Watson looked at her in amazement. She waddled her way up to Dan, nosed in his pocket, pulled out the fish and swallowed it. Tom Watson could hardly believe his eyes when he saw Dan patting and stroking her.

"Will it let me touch it?" he asked Dan and reached out a hand towards Grace's shoulder, but in doing so, he accidentally trod on her flipper. She turned and snapped at him and Tom jumped back in a panic.

"I don't think she likes you," Dan said loftily, rubbing the top of Grace's head.

"Why not?"

"Maybe she doesn't like transistors. Maybe she prefers a mouth-organ," Dan said with a happy inspiration.

Tom Watson tuned in his transistor again, but obligingly

Grace turned and snarled at him and Tom backed away and switched off.

"Let me have a go with your mouth-organ, Dan," he asked persuasively.

"What? After all you've said about it? No fear! This thing's got *magic*."

Dan played another few bars of Grace's tune and walked up and down the beach. Grace hauled herself along after him, now and again rubbing her nose affectionately against him.

Now Tom Watson really did begin to believe in the magic of the mouth-organ and he longed like anything to possess it.

"Will you swop your mouth-organ for my hand-torch?" he asked Dan.

"I've got a perfectly good hand-torch of my own," Dan said with contempt.

Tom Watson was driven to foolish desperation. "Then will you swop it for my transistor?"

"Never!" Dan declared. "You couldn't play my mouth-organ, anyway. All you can do is switch a knob to make music come out of that box. No seal would ever come out of the water for that! I'll keep my mouth-organ, thanks!"

Tom Watson had no answer. He looked at Dan with a new respect, even with a shiver of awe. Dan Reid had the power to charm a seal out of the water! At that moment Grace took it into her head to turn and snarl again at Tom. He hastily retreated, turned on his heel and made for the upper path. If Dan could have seen, the tears were not far from Tom Watson's eyes.

Dan was left alone on the beach with Grace. He petted her for a few minutes and they both stared out to sea in the direction of the Farne Islands. Then it was as if a summons came to the seal. She gave a last loving pat to Dan's hand with her flipper, then hauled herself down into the water, splashed her way through the shallows and began swimming. Dan watched her till her head became a speck in the distance, but she did not look back. He raised his mouth-organ to his lips, then, without playing a note, he dropped it again. The hot tears ran down his face. All at once he found his grandfather beside him.

"Grandma sent me after you, Dan," he said quietly. "She saw Tom Watson go away and watched you playing with the seal till she swam away. Has Grace gone?"

Dan pointed speechlessly at the tiny speck heading for the open sea.

"It had to come, Dan lad. It's the call of her own folk. She's gone out to her own world now, just as some day you must go out too."

"*I* must? You mean when I go to that school on the mainland?"

"Yes, Dan. And perhaps some day even further than the school on the mainland. Life may call you to far places, but when you go, go bravely without a backward look, like your seal did."

"I'll remember," Dan said. "But I'll never forget my island."

"Grandma said I was to tell you that your seal would never forget about you and the island either, Dan. Some day, when she's a mother-seal herself, she'll bring her baby to Lindisfarne to show you. Your Grandma knows about seals."

"Yes, she knows about seals," Dan repeated in a quiet confident voice. "And she knows we shall both come back to Lindisfarne, however far we go."

## SOME USEFUL BOOKS

*Grey Seals and the Farne Islands*, by Grace Hickling

*A Seal Flies By*, by R. H. Pearson

*       *       *

*Lindisfarne*, by R. A. and D. B. Cartwright—this is by far
   the most recent and fullest account of the island

*The Lindisfarne Story*, by Charles Cromarty

*Holy Island (Lindisfarne)*, by Charles Cromarty—a holiday
   guidebook

*Holy Island*, by Frank Graham—a guidebook

*A Naturalist on Lindisfarne*, by Richard Perry

*Highways and Byways of Northumbria*

# SOME USEFUL DATES

643–5 A.D.    The Christian king of Northumberland asks for missionaries from Iona to convert his pagan people: St Aidan and a group of monks come south in answer, and choose Lindisfarne as the site of their monastery: from this base, St Aidan goes on foot through Northumberland, converting all its people: he becomes the first Bishop of Lindisfarne

At about this time, a shepherd boy called Cuthbert is living in the Border hills

651    St Aidan dies: Cuthbert enters the monastery of Melrose, under one of Aidan's disciples, with whom he later goes to Lindisfarne where he takes up the life of a hermit

676–85    St Cuthbert lives a life of solitary prayer in a hermit's hut which he builds on the Farne Islands

685    St Cuthbert reluctantly agrees to become Bishop of Lindisfarne

687        St Cuthbert returns to his Farne Island retreat
           and dies there: his body is carried to Lindis-
           farne for burial: the first pilgrims come to pray
           at his tomb

700        At about this time, the beautiful Lindisfarne
           Gospels are created

793        Danish pirates plunder the island, burn the
           Abbey and kill several of the monks: St Cuth-
           bert's tomb is undisturbed.

           Within ten years, the Abbey is rebuilt

875        Threat of new Danish invasion: monks leave
           the island, taking with them the Lindisfarne
           Gospels, St Cuthbert's body, and several other
           treasures: the monastery abandoned

1066       William the Conqueror, Duke of Normandy,
           invades England and makes himself king:
           Northumbria holds out against him

1069       William's army lays waste the north country:
           monks from St Cuthbert's shrine in Durham
           retreat for safety to Lindisfarne, taking his body
           with them

1070       Monks return to Durham

1082       The church of Lindisfarne is given by the
           Bishop of Durham to the Durham Benedictine
           convent of monks: with Durham as their
           mother house, they set up a small community
           there under a prior

| | |
|---|---|
| 1090 | Monks rename Lindisfarne "Holy Island" |
| 1093 | Work begins on Priory church |
| 1100 | Building of Parish church begins about this time |
| 1344 | Monks establish the quarrying of limestone as island industry |
| 1372 | At about this time, monks build boats and encourage herring fishing |
| 1537–50 | Henry VIII reforms the Church in England and dissolves the monasteries, among them the Holy Island priory |
| 1539–50 | Threat of Scottish invasion: the island is used as a Navy base, against the Scots: castle built on Beblowe crag: garrison established |
| 1675 | Fort built on Steel End |
| 1792 | First mining for coal |
| 1821 | Castle garrison disbanded |
| 1826 | Lighthouse erected on Farne Islands |
| 1838 | Grace Darling and her father rescue survivors from wreck of *Forfarshire* |
| 1839 | First lifeboat house built |

1850          Dundee company expands lime quarrying
              Herring fisheries flourish

1900          Closing of the lime kilns
              Herring fisheries shut down: boats turned into
              fishermen's sheds